see
how
small

see
how
small

A NOVEL

SCOTT BLACKWOOD

(L) (B)

Little, Brown and Company

New York • Boston • London

Little, Brown and Company
Hachette Book Group
1290 Avenue of the Americas, New York, NY 10104
littlebrown.com

First Edition: January 2015

Little, Brown and Company is a division of Hachette Book Group, Inc. The Little, Brown name and logo are trademarks of Hachette Book Group, Inc.

The publisher is not responsible for websites (or their content) that are not owned by the publisher.

The Hachette Speakers Bureau provides a wide range of authors for speaking events. To find out more, go to hachettespeakersbureau.com or call (866) 376-6591.

ISBN 978-0-316-37380-7
LCCN 2014944785

10 9 8 7 6 5 4 3 2 1

RRD-C

Printed in the United States of America

For Ava, Ellie & Tommi

The first time I heard the voice I was terrified. It was noon, in summer, in my father's garden. . . . I seldom heard the voice when it was not accompanied by a light. Usually it was very bright.

—JOAN OF ARC, FROM THE TRANSCRIPT OF HER TRIAL

Thomas Aquinas invented a third order of duration distinct from time and eternity, which he called aevum. . . . It co-exists with temporal events, at the moment of occurrence, being, as was said, like a stick in a river. Aevum, you might say, is the time order of novels.

—FRANK KERMODE, THE SENSE OF AN ENDING

It shall be called "Bottom's Dream," because it hath no bottom.

—NICK BOTTOM, IN WILLIAM SHAKESPEARE'S
A MIDSUMMER NIGHT'S DREAM

I

1

WE HAVE ALWAYS lived here, though we pretend we've just arrived. That's the trick, to make forgetful shapes with your mouth so everything feels new and unremembered. But after a while we slip up. A careless word, an uninvited smell, a tip-of-the-tongue taste of something sweet, makes the room suddenly familiar—and we have to begin again. Like startled infants, we look to your face to tell us what comes next. You came into the fire.

Take off your clothes, the men with guns said.

Please, we said.

Now, they said.

Please let us go, we said. We won't tell anyone.

Not anyone? They smiled with their guns.

Not anyone, we said. Please.

Our jeans and boots and jackets and shirts were piled high in the middle of the floor, like a breaking wave.

The tile was cold under our feet.

Across the room, the stainless-steel ice cream case gleamed. On the floor beside it, the cash register drawer sprawled on its side.

What a shame, our mothers said from somewhere, no time to tidy up.

Before the men with guns bound and gagged us with our own bras and panties right after closing time, a few things happened: one of us hid inside her mouth the opal class ring her boyfriend had given her and remembered her mother singing "Sweet Baby James" and stroking her forehead when she had her migraines. The youngest of us, who always threw up before gym class because she was afraid of being naked, realized that this time she wouldn't. Another remembered the pride she'd felt the day before, riding a horse no one in her family could ride, a horse that had thrown her older sister. He knows your true heart, her father had said. The horse's shoulders were lathered with sweat. He had a salty, earthy smell she'd thought of as love.

The men with guns did things to us.

Afterward, our cheeks against the tile, we could smell something in the air like our own blood. Then lighter fluid. Burning plastic. Flames climbed the walls, flashed over the ceiling. Eventually the pipes above us burst.

Our mothers wore disappointed faces.

We waited for a voice.

We waited for a light.

Near the dumped-over register drawer, a bed-wetting nine-year-old boy we'd all babysat one time or another appeared. Nicholas. He smelled like sandalwood soap and pee. He would lie to us about brushing his teeth. He would walk in on us in the bathroom, where there wasn't a lock. What are you doing here? we demanded. His stealthy blue eyes gazed back. You must be cold, he said to us on the floor. Where are your clothes?

4

He pretended not to know they were burning. Nicholas. Some things never change.

It grew hot, dark, and wet like first things.

But then you came into the fire. Found us. In all that dark and smoke and water: a bright, bare foot. The hopeful turn of an ankle. You clothed us in light. Washed our hair.

Instead of nothing, we have you.

2

KATE'S TWO DAUGHTERS are working behind the counter of the ice cream shop Kate and her ex-husband once owned. The girls wear robin's-egg-blue polo shirts with SANDRA'S—Kate's mother's name—stitched in gold across their chests, their name tags just above. The girls are bird-breasted, Kate thinks, but not wispy, not fragile. Their hair—Elizabeth's dark, Zadie's coffee and milk—pulled back in ponytails, which makes the freckled slope of their foreheads and noses more pronounced, like Kate's. The girls are talking to customers—wide-eyed, polite attentiveness for the adults; rolled-eyed smirking for the languid, horse-faced boys from their high school, shambling in line. Elizabeth, Kate's younger daughter, at the front register, her face roiled with the first joys of being noticed and confusion over change amounts. Zadie, distant-eyed and aloof, at the drive-through window, leaning out into the shadowy late afternoon. Half swallowed up, Kate thinks, like an offering.

The ice cream shop smells of waffle cones. After their late shifts, the girls bring home this smell pleated in their clothes and hair—how they hate it, this baked-in dark sweetness. *Conefication,* they call it. Before bed, the girls will try scrubbing it from their skin. But to Kate—lying fitfully in the dark alongside her sleeping then-husband Ray—it's the smell of gratefulness. All day, she's fasted on the girls' absence. And now the thick, sugary smell of them is everywhere. Slowly, slowly, she cautions herself. The starved can only take in so much at once.

Some of Kate's friends think the girls are standoffish, too much in their own heads, troubled. Those Ulrich girls, they say. Kate knows this. There are whispers about her permissiveness, about drive-through window bartering of wine coolers and rum for sundaes and shakes. Grass-fire rumors about older boys and mushrooms in Zilker Park (conjured up, she suspects, by Sarah Haven, whose son was hauled off to alternative school and whose husband sleeps with men). The girls have tested Kate, it's true. There was the time Zadie was caught shoplifting cosmetics. Pink coral lipstick. Or was it condoms? Kate decides it was both for continuity's sake.

Now out in the ice cream shop parking lot, the last of the sun flares off car hoods. A chill is settling in. Some of the dropouts and hangers-on clown and take photos in front of Hollis Finger's beat-up art car, its roof and hood tattooed with a mosaic of seashells, buttons, beads, metal army men, and hairless dolls. Hollis Finger, who because of a wartime head injury can't find the mental thread on which to string the everyday beads of his life, looks out with indigestion at the scene from one of the shop's cramped tables.

Meredith—Mare, the girls call her, because of her horse riding and sometimes, it's true, because of her incisors, which jut at odd angles—walks in through the front door fifteen minutes late. Zadie looks over from the drive-through. Elizabeth smirks. Meredith—her mind in full gallop—has forgotten her SANDRA'S shirt. She makes wide eyes at the girls, meaning, of course, that she has a secret. Maneuvers through the line, then around the end of the counter, ties an apron around her waist. Zadie says, I hope it was worth it, and slams the drive-through register drawer closed as if Meredith's finger is inside.

Then, for some reason, most likely because Kate Ulrich is embellishing, revising even as she reimagines it, the parking lot goes dark. Days are shorter now, Kate thinks. Winter closing in. The girls' summery arms and sunshine feet growing paler. Soon everyone in line will rush off to day-care pickup, soccer practice, dinner, or dates. Kate knows many of them, knows they weren't really gathered here on this day, at this early-evening hour, but it seems right somehow. Meredith's father, who owns a horse ranch west of town and a real estate agency that Kate will later work for, waves at Meredith from the front. He holds up the SANDRA's shirt she left behind on the kitchen table at home. Beside him, Rosa Heller, a newspaper reporter, hunches her shoulders to hide her six-foot height. Nearby, twirling her hair with her fingers, Margo Farbrother, who has discovered—against all odds—a child hidden in the folds of her fibroid-filled uterus. Jack Dewey, a firefighter who lives in Kate's neighborhood, whose daughter, Sam, has gone missing. Jack will soon be tethered to Kate by an invisible cord and anchored to this very spot.

There is a young man in line Kate doesn't know. Smooth-shaven, his face pale and round, hands jammed in the pockets of an elegant gray wool overcoat. Something vintage. Later, he'll be described as secretive and nervous, but this won't be right. The young man insists that others go ahead of him, says that he's *undecided*. The wool overcoat is too big in the shoulders, oversize in the cuffs, so the young man seems smaller than he is. Maybe even younger than he is. In fact, he doesn't seem to have an age. His skin is creaseless but you can see the adult in his eyes. *Who's in there?* Kate wonders. *I'm undecided,* he says again, and gestures toward the counter as if he were an usher showing them to seats at a performance. There is something gallant about the coat and gesture, Kate thinks. Something ageless and chivalrous that pleases her, but also leaves her cold. Maybe his eyes.

I'm undecided.

Aren't we all, she thinks.

Then waffle cone batter is burning on the griddle. Black smoke billows where the vegetable oil has spilled. The customer in the wool overcoat, now sipping a shake, asks in his gallant, undecided way if something is burning. Jack Dewey, our firefighter, leaps over the counter and grabs wet rags, smothers the smoldering acrid sweetness. The girls use spatulas to toss the blackened mass into the sink, but burn their fingertips anyway. Zadie, who's worked here the longest, has several small crescent-shaped burn scars on the heel of her palm and wrist.

Now, because of the smoke, it's dark inside and out. The young man in the wool overcoat throws open the receiving doors in back; another customer props open the front. Smoke dissipates. Everyone laughs nervously. Someone claps Jack on the back. The girls fidget behind the counter, as if they've been caught at a failed imitation of adults, as if they'd gotten drunk on the fumes, being so close. They imagine being spoken about in the crowd. Shame washes over them momentarily. Something surges in Kate. She longs for the girls to steal kisses, to drink just a little to quiet their nerves, to seize whatever they can of this life, to feel they are bound for something bigger, something beyond what everyone imagines they're bound for.

Then the girls reenter their bodies, those unpredictable inventions, and with still-summery arms they wipe down the front counters and ask who is next.

3

WHAT IS JACK Dewey thinking before he goes into the fire?

1. Of his nylon search rope, which is five-sixteenths of an inch in diameter and two hundred feet long and attached to a snap hook on his belt. How Neftali Rodriguez and Henry Soto will expect him to deploy it, given the ice cream shop's mazelike conditions and intense smoke.

2. That they will not need the rope because he knows this is likely an arson fire to collect the insurance money—like so many others lately—and there will be no one in the building to search for.

3. That he's forgotten to tie the knots in the nylon search rope at fifteen-foot intervals, which tell you how far you have to go to exit the building. How much shit he will catch for this will depend on Neftali's and Henry's moods. But there will be significant shit to catch.

4. He thinks—even as he and Henry Soto pull open the blackened double front doors of the ice cream shop and the smoke and heat hit them like a blow to the chest and then coils upward—of his failure as a father. Thinks of his sixteen-year-old daughter,

Sam, running away three weeks ago and how he hasn't been able to find her, despite the missing persons report, despite his several friends on the police force. He sees Sam barefoot in her capris in some strange kitchen, frying catfish in a pan, like they sometimes did on Fridays. One of the traditions he'd carried on after his wife died. He tries not to think of the prick of a boyfriend she's likely with, who smells pungently moist like bong smoke and carries around a little metal tackle box of harmonicas in different keys and can't play a lick.

5. Heading into the fire, the safety rope trailing behind, he thinks instead: Friday night. If Sam were back, she might even have come by here for an ice cream cone, then out with friends to a movie or the improv comedy club downtown. She'd call him from the lobby and say in a deflated voice that plans had changed, that she really needed a ride home. *Please?* He'd know that she was near tears. A tightness would rise up in his chest and he'd say, without exasperation or fear, *I'm on my way.*

4

HOLLIS FINGER, SITTING at a back table in the ice cream shop, can tell before he looks up from his crossword that the man is hideous.

But that's a little later.

At the moment, Hollis is watching one of the dropout boys out in the parking lot pry loose a medium-size conch shell—a *Strombus gigas* he prizes for its depth of color—from the hood of his art car. Hollis wants to twist off a table leg and beat the boy. Around him, at the other tables, heads swivel. He suspects he's yelled an obscenity, maybe even a threat. He removes his hand from the table leg. Tries to smile to put everyone at ease, but he can taste the bile at the back of his throat. He focuses on his chocolate-dipped cone. Licks it tentatively. The whole shop smells of his anxiety. He closes his eyes a moment to calm himself. Sees the boy's limp body on the pavement, his splayed, upturned palm. The conch. Its rosy insides like last light. But one of its horns is broken off. There's a roaring in Hollis's ears.

Sir? Someone touches his shoulder. He flinches, fumbles his dipped cone to the floor. It's a hideous ruin on the tile. Separated into three parts. Incompatible. A fringed spatter of chocolate outlines the body.

Sir? It's one of the counter girls. He's noticed her before. She wears a flesh-colored hearing aid in her right ear, though you can barely see it. He wonders if she hears the same roaring he does. She has a large nose. Healthy nostrils. Elastic skin. She smells of high school hallways.

Are you okay? She asks this softly. She looks him over. Some of the people around him are still glancing his way, interested. Maybe protective.

He looks down at the ruin of his cone. Out to the parking lot, his car, the boy, the conch. Shadows falling. *I'm just dandy,* he says, near tears.

The girl, after some discussions with her associates, replaces his cone with a double. When she comes by and presents it to him— *Voila, monsieur,* she says—he notices a series of curved shapes, raised hieroglyphics along the inside of her wrist. He gently touches her there, the smooth elasticity of her skin. *I will not forget you,* he thinks. *I've carved you on the palm of my hand.*

She smiles at him as if she knows Isaiah by heart.

What did this hideous man look like? the detectives ask him later (how much later Hollis can't say). He tries to describe him to the well-groomed sketch artist they've brought in, just the basics, the feel of the hideous man's presence. He thinks of the disquieting sheen of the black buttons on the man's coat. The man's older companion tapping out a song on a table with a plastic spoon.

The light in the little room gives everything a greenish tint, like the air before a storm. Hollis can't get it right. The detectives sigh and bully him. One throws a pencil at the wall and it makes a *ka-tic* sound. They send the sketch artist away. Finally, Hollis says something—not about the hideous man, but about the boy and the conch in the parking lot, the grievous injury to his car—and the detectives' eyes grow bright. They ask him to concentrate. *Can you draw the man in the long coat, the one who stood in line? Can you do that for us, Mr. Finger?*

The hideous man, Hollis says.

Yes, the hideous man.

Hollis can hear yelling in another small room somewhere. A silverfish flits at the edge of his vision. He shuffles the drawing paper. One of the detectives picks up the pencil off the floor. When Hollis has finished the drawing, the detectives lean over him, block the light with their bodies. Finally they say, *Look, Mr. Finger, what you've drawn here is a nostril, and here you've depicted in detail the skin flap of an eyelid.*

There's no pleasing some people, Hollis thinks.

5

MICHAEL GREER IS seventeen. He's sitting in an idling Volvo wagon behind the ice cream shop with the headlights off. He's the lookout and driver. The car is stolen and they've switched the plates. It's cold out, but the windows are down because he's sweating. His mouth is dry. He popped two tabs of Vicodin a little while ago to calm his nerves. The night presses close but drifts away at the edges. A pecan tree looms above the car. Every time the wind picks up, a few pecans plunk loudly off the roof.

The two men inside the shop are calmly purposeful. Michael hates the older one already for his cracks about Michael's clothes and hygiene. The two men will torch the place. Someone somewhere gets the insurance payout. Michael gets a small cut. Nothing too complicated. No one gets hurt. His job earlier was to watch from across the street: the shop girls turning up chairs on tabletops, the shop girls counting the register drawers, the shop girls mopping the floor. Then the lights went down; a little later, the front door opened and he thought he could hear their singsong voices. Much later, it will occur to Michael that he should have seen in the two men's measured strides, in their coiled energy, even in their acceptance of him, something else.

He doesn't know the two men's names. They don't know his. That's one of the rules. He knows he's on the bottom rung of this thing. But he senses that for the first time he's working with real adults who mean something in the world, who know what risk is and how to manage it. *So can we count on you?* the younger man in the gray wool overcoat asked over dinner at Fran's Hamburgers the night before. He said it as if it was hardly worth the asking. A formality. He was kind and attentive, even if the clothes he wore were out of date. A funny slender tie, a wool overcoat in a style Michael had seen in old movies. The younger man's face was smooth and pale, and Michael thought he'd probably never had acne but could understand the trials of those who had. He'd asked if Michael was working on his GED and Michael lied. The older man, whose hair was thinning, laughed ruefully and said, *Sure, that's you. Overachiever.* The younger man tilted his head in a disappointed way as if a favorite uncle said something racist at the dinner table. Then the younger man had asked the girl bussing tables about the photographs of local celebrities on the wall as if it meant the world to him to know all about them. The girl had a nice smile and Michael realized that it was the young man's guileless face that drew the smile out of her. His undivided attention. His voice, a gentle plumbing of her depths.

The two men told him they'd be inside the ice cream shop ten minutes tops, but they are edging into twenty already. A wave of nausea breaks over him and passes. He hadn't eaten before taking the pills. He feels in his jacket pocket for his cigarettes and finds the conch shell. He'd broken it off the art car earlier when they were casing the shop and the art car man had tried to tackle him in the parking lot. Knocked him back against a car hood. The

17

man had blubbered and sobbed, making no sense. Michael punched him. Busted his lip. Chipped a tooth. One of the ice cream shop girls, tall, freckled, had come out to calm down the art car man. A Mexican-looking girl passed a bag of ice through the drive-through window for his mouth. A few random people from the parking lot bunched around them, not knowing what to do. The art car man blubbered to Michael about returning the shell to its legal and rightful owner. His teeth were flecked with blood. "Shame on you," the freckled girl said, turning to Michael. "Shame." Michael stammered out something about self-defense. The girl said, "Just look at what you did." Michael shrugged. "He started it," Michael said, feeling small. He glanced around at unfamiliar faces, felt his own flush with hatred and embarrassment. The parking lot seemed to stretch out in the twilight. The girl's eyes burned. Standing on the curb, holding the ice pack to the art car man's mouth, she had a kind of self-righteous grace that made Michael want to kiss her and hit her all at once.

Above the Volvo, pecan branches lace low, silvered clouds. A billboard for a radio station with a large lipstick kiss rises over the florist shop next door. Michael lights a cigarette, examines the conch shell under the lighter flame. He decides that it looks like a vagina. Its undulating pink folds. He tries to put it out of his mind, tries to concentrate on the back roads he's memorized, the drop-off street for the car. *A job well done,* he hears the younger man tell him. He claps Michael on the shoulder, hands him a beer. Even the older man Michael hates is impressed. *Never flinched,* he says. *I was dead wrong about you.* The younger man gives him a look that bridges the gap between them until it hardly seems there at all. *You are not a child,* the look says. And then—and the change is only noticeable at the drifting edges of things — it's not the young man at all but Michael's dead brother, Andrew. He's sitting on top of a picnic table near the pecan tree, a hand pressed to his face where his jaw used to be before he was shot. It's a tender moment, Michael thinks, Andrew thinking of him while he thinks of Andrew. Blood summoning blood. Concern flickers over Andrew's half face. Then he smiles with what he has left, smooths out the edges. *Well, look at you,* he says. He walks to the car, bums a cigarette from Michael. Andrew fumbles a bit to find the corner of his mouth, lights his own cigarette from Michael's. Steps back in a kind of appraisal. Michael still remembers him like this, shambling and slouchy, in a movie antihero kind of way.

You are one doomed motherfucker, Andrew says matter-of-factly.

In the dim glow of the shop's back door light, his fleshy opening looks like the raw insides of the conch shell. Michael is thinking of the implications of this, Andrew's return, his own seething hatred and love for his brother's absence, when he hears the first muffled gunshots inside the ice cream shop.

6

A T THE FRONT door, one of the officers tells Kate that there's been a fire. Their breath streams in the porch light. Kate thinks of the small fire at the ice cream shop earlier, the acrid burnt sweetness. Smoke. How it is hardly worth the drive over to tell her this.

"Where are my girls?" she asks.

"Can we come inside, Ms. Ulrich?" the second officer asks, his body hunched against the cold, but also against something imminent. Something that hasn't happened yet, she thinks, but will when it leaves his smoking mouth. She resolves not to listen.

"Who's at the door, Kate?" her husband, Ray, the girls' stepfather, yells from the bedroom. She can hear the jangle of Ray's belt buckle as he lifts his pants from the foot of the bed and pulls them on. In his pockets, the keys to the ice cream shop, where he'd stopped by just after closing to pick up the night deposit. A movie, he'd said when he got back home late and crawled into bed. The girls were headed to a midnight movie after locking up at eleven. "Didn't you ask them which movie?" Kate had said, because you always ask which one, always. Good old feckless Ray. She lay there beside him, blood drumming in her head, listening to his raspy breathing, thinking, *I will go away. When the girls finally leave home, I will leave home too.* Then, a little later, after she'd tried their cell phones and gotten their chirpy voice mail greetings, Kate woke startled from a dream in which her dead mother was combing her hair with an ear of corn. She couldn't smell the girls in the house.

At the front door, the first police officer tells her something brutally quiet and small about her daughters. Something so dense that it makes everything—the cold, smoking air, the officers' ashen faces, Ray's raspy breathing—constrict to a singular point.

Past the officers framed in the doorway she can see the squad car outside, its headlights illuminating the cedar tree beside the driveway. In the fogged back windows, she thinks she can make out Elizabeth and Zadie, their bare feet propped on the metal grill between the seats. Cocksure, dismissive. Playing the parts assigned to them. Certain they can talk their way out of anything.

7

AFTER FINDING THE dead girls in the fire, Jack Dewey didn't know what to think. At first, he seemed mostly fine, having gone to see a department-provided therapist for a few months. Bad dreams and cold sweats were nothing unusual, the therapist told him. It was a process he'd need to work through. The firefighters at his station seemed to understand his woodenness at work and offered encouragement—a few of them had been on tours in Iraq and seen bad things happen. Whole families burned. Children's arms, legs, heads, blown off. But to Jack, this all happened in vast, incomprehensible cities and deserts, places with guttural-sounding names he'd never visit. Still, several of the firefighters made sure, on his four days off a week, to check in or invite him to play softball with some city league team that needed a sub, or to grab a beer in the evening. They had done this too after his wife died ten years before, in his second year with the department. They'd made an effort to fix him up with blind dates—usually nervous, mid-thirties friends of their wives or girlfriends, who had decided they were too old for the music clubs or didn't like online dating sites.

But things had not gotten better after the fire—if *better* meant getting along with his girlfriend, Carla, and his daughter, Sam, or having a few moments of stillness in his mind. He often drank at Deep Eddy Bar until he couldn't feel his face, and would wobble home on his bike down the expressway shoulder. This was after the DUI, when he'd fallen asleep in the car while idling in line at Mrs. Johnson's Donuts. Now he'd occasionally glimpse himself in the bar mirror, his hands adjusting his helmet for the ride home. His head gargantuan and grotesque. Whose head and face were these? He often thought now, nearly five years later, how the firefighters at his station, or even the detectives on the case who'd questioned him, thought he was drinking to forget the girls. But the truth was, the more he drank, the more stove-in he became on the outside, the more inwardly alive he felt. He doesn't see the images of the girls' naked burned bodies anymore, as he once did, stacked upon one another, their open opaque eyes staring at nothing. He doesn't wake up on fire and thrash in the bed, frantically trying to rip off his burning helmet and airpack. Once he'd flung his arms so violently that he'd broken Carla's nose. Carla, out of sheer terror, had begun to toss a quilt over him and pretend to smother the fire, and sometimes that would break the spell. He'd gone to see a therapist again after the broken nose, trying to restore some trust between them. Over the past five years, though, the dreams had become more vivid, sharper around the edges, and, to his great shame, even more real to him than memories of his dead wife. To his astonishment and confusion, in these dreams he sees, and even speaks to, the girls from the fire, as they would be now, five years later, in their early twenties, near the same age as his daughter.

*   *   *

"What kind of dad are you?" Jack's daughter, Sam, said into the phone in a voice that seemed to understand exactly the kind of dad he was. He'd said some things, accused her of some things he shouldn't have. This was four months after she'd come back home, a year and a half after the fire. She was calling him from Brackenridge Hospital to tell him she and her boyfriend had had a wreck. Sam was a little banged up — some cuts from the glass. The new boyfriend had a concussion. But when the cops and EMS crew found his pickup in the culvert, they also discovered some cellophane-wrapped hashish stuffed into the fingers of a single leather glove in the console. Now the boyfriend needed an attorney and some bail money.

"I guess I'm the kind of dad who comes when you need me," he said on the phone, trying on a kind of casual bluster because, as she often pointed out, he was afraid of her.

Later, in the emergency room, he sat near a large tinted window and could feel the day's heat through the glass. Another man sat nearby, cupping his limp arm at the elbow as if cradling an infant's head. He signed in at the desk and a pregnant Hispanic nurse wearing slippers helped him navigate the maze of cubicle rooms.

Sam was born in this hospital. She'd developed an infection from breathing meconium during a long, difficult delivery, so they'd put her in the neonatal ICU for two weeks to treat it, strapped a tangle of wires to her chest and head to monitor her vitals. She was stout compared with the other babies there. Premies not any bigger than potatoes — they were even swaddled in aluminum foil to keep their heat in. It scared him to think something so tiny could still be a human being. Some of them had been there for months because of heart ailments, kidney problems, or congenital defects that wouldn't allow them to breathe on their own. The terrible, contingent life of these infants, the wires, the constant beeping and buzzing alarms, warning of some impending failure, made him constantly on edge. Everything in the neonatal ICU—a room festooned with the false cheer of newborn blues and pinks—seemed to partially negate the future. The thought of Sam forever dependent on machines and nurses and catheters made his throat constrict at night. He heard her raw-throat crying in his dreams. His wife, recovering in a nearby room from a torn cervix, would ask him for a report after the midnight feeding. "How's our sweet baby girl?" she'd ask from beneath the tide of sedatives. "Dreaming of her momma," he'd say.

A number of the premies wouldn't survive. An intern had told him this while eating a sandwich at the nurses' station. There was a point at which the parents—often sleep deprived, living in a fog—had to make a decision. Jack also remembered the hospital chaplain, a chain smoker, telling him that one of the premies his heart malformed and too weak for surgery—had completely baffled the neonatologists. Miraculously, the chaplain said, his body had "learned" to reroute his oxygenated blood to his brain through a system of collateral arteries. But to Jack this seemed only a reprieve, a story of deferred grief that made the later one even harder to bear. He remembered his grandfather's stories of families during the 1918 flu pandemic waiting to name their children until it was clear they'd make it to their first birthday. When Jack would take bottles of his wife's breast milk into the

25

ICU to feed Sam, he'd see the parents of the critical premies coming and going in their ill-fitting visitor scrubs, their bright, hag-
gard faces. They seemed like castaways who didn't know they'd
been abandoned. And seven years later, in the weeks leading up to
his wife's death from a brain aneurysm, he knew he'd worn that
same expression on his pilgrimages. He'd made any bargain,
buoyed any false hope, explained away, even at the end, the inevitable signs of his wife's body shutting down.

Jack knew now that luck was unearned—arbitrary, even. But
in the ICU with his daughter those early weeks, surrounded
by premies swaddled in aluminum foil, he'd studied the tiny
maps of capillaries on Sam's eyelids and considered himself a
fortunate man.

In the emergency room, Jack found Sam tucked away in one of the
cubicles, sitting on the lip of the bed. He hugged her before she
could get up, and she stiffened, then gave in. She was shaking.

"It's just the adrenaline after the accident," he said. "It goes on
awhile." She held up a trembling hand and laughed. Shiny flecks
of glass were embedded in the reddened skin below her knuckles.

Jack's heart rattled in his chest to see her scared.

She looked at him. "The deer just leaped out in the road."

"How fast were you going?"

"Not fast. No faster than normal."

"Were you smoking hash?"

"Jesus. Dad. No."

"I have to ask that."

"You don't have to ask."

"Where did the stuff in the console come from?"

"Who knows—one of Adrian's friends, probably."

"The one-handed man."

"I have broken glass in *my* hand." She waved it in front of him.

"It should be a reminder," he said, and thought of her plunging headfirst through the windshield, hair and blood. His legs weakened.

"Is that what you tell burned people? This should be a reminder?"

"If they're the ones who started the fire, sure."

She was suddenly silent, and he knew she was thinking of the ice cream shop. He leaned forward and kissed the top of Sam's head. She'd always been lucky. Always favored. Which made him worry all the more.

8

THIS IS WHAT Rosa Heller, a reporter covering the murders for the *Chronicle,* remembers: She's seven years old, walking hand in hand with her dad toward the Lab School on the South Side of Chicago. She's tall for her age, and in fifth grade she'll begin to slouch to hide it. It's early morning, still, and a fog off Lake Michigan clings to the yards and stoops. They stop at a corner grocery that sells the Wacky Packages stickers that she's obsessed with, and her father gives her money to buy some because she loves him so much. When they turn the corner they walk alongside a vacant lot with a billboard for NuGrape soda and beneath it there's a large blackened oval in the grass where someone set a fire. She wonders who would do something like that and decides that boys would, just to see what happened. She sees something shiny in the grass that she thinks is a bottle cap for her collection, and so pulls away from her dad and scuffs the dirt and grass with her shoe. She finds a half-dollar-size hoop earring. In the weeds near a metal fence, not twenty feet away, she sees a mustard-colored jacket. Then a brown leather purse, a string of toiletries, a pair of panties, a hair pick, and a compact mirror. Near the compact mirror, a brown hand that once held it. At first Rosa thinks the face staring back from a clump of weeds is a

Halloween mask. She looks at her dad to be in on the joke, but he just stares. She can feel her skin prickle, but it takes a while for her to realize that it's a woman's face, missing nose and ears.

Rosa's dad, Peter, was a politics reporter for the *Chicago Tribune*. They lived with her mother in a partly rehabbed two-flat surrounded by run-down rentals, used car lots, and liquor stores. The area was segregated, but a number of liberal white families, like hers, had moved into it in the late sixties, even given all the turbulence. Even partly because of it. Her parents had participated in freedom marches and seen violence up close. Her dad had had his nose broken. Someone had hit her mother in the head with a D-cell battery. On her dad's desk at the *Tribune* she remembered a photo of him between the writer Alex Haley and the actor and activist Ossie Davis, smiling broadly.

Occasionally in their neighborhood someone would overturn a car and set it on fire, which secretly thrilled Rosa—she could often see the glow from her upstairs bedroom window. Her dad took great pains to explain to her that this was a symptom of an illness. Like the chicken pox or a rash? she asked. That's right, her dad said, a warning on the surface about what was going on inside. There was so much anger that maybe it couldn't be contained. Better a car than a passerby, he said. Better things than a person.

She doesn't think it happened that way. Her dad wouldn't have allowed her to get so close to the dead woman. She would have heard about the nose and ears most likely from someone at school, or maybe her dad talking to one of the local politicos on the phone. Or possibly she'd imagined it. She'd even looked in the *Tribune* archives to find the story, but couldn't find any mention of mutilation. She wondered if this was like her memory of her dad one day cutting the TV power cord with a pair of gleaming shears while she was watching it, or the time she was forced to leave for summer camp while her Labrador, Ali, was dying on the living room floor—memories she suspected she made up to confirm what she already believed about her dad. Some lack in him. What had she believed? That he was high-principled but cruel. A gifted journalist who abused his talent. A secret racist who helped black people so that he could feel better about bitter feelings he harbored against them. He was guileless to a fault. He'd eventually driven off Rosa's mother with his various lost causes and under-the-table funding of his younger brother, Bill, who was constantly strung out on back pain medicine and running from creditors. Much of what she'd accepted about her dad when she was younger she was unsure about now, which had both helped and hurt their relationship, she suspected. She can see her dad's hands, their neatly trimmed, milky nails, the lump on the outside of his left hand where a benign tumor made the bone brittle and caused him to break the hand half a dozen times. How could the tumor be benign, she wondered, if it ate away the bone? On a recent visit to Chicago, she'd asked him if he'd had his checkup, his scheduled colonoscopy and PSA blood work. He said to be honest, he couldn't remember when he'd last seen a doctor. He smiled a little boy's smile that pretended not to know. On the table in front of her, his left hand seemed frail, the lump more pronounced. She loved his guileless eyes, the way they took in everything and denied it all.

*   *   *

It would have happened this way: Her dad takes her hand, leads her away from the vacant lot and the dead woman. Rosa never sees what she thinks she did—holes where the woman's nose and ears should be. Voids. The woman's skirt hiked up, the greenish glass of the Coke bottle stuck between her legs. When Rosa begins pointing near the fence, her dad makes light of what they see there, someone asleep in the weeds. *Siesta time,* he'd say, then make a snoring sound and pull Rosa away. The woman's body sprawled languidly on the ground as if she were in her own bed and not a vacant lot. Her compact mirror open beside her, a quick powder touch-up when she wakes. *Lazy bones,* Rosa's dad would say. *Get up and get on your way. Don't stray from the path. Don't tarry.*

He would have protected her.

9

HOLLIS OFTEN CONFUSES what's already happened with what's to come. He knows this. Still, they feel the same.

The light was like a sudden blow to the head. It filled the interior of Hollis's art car, made night into day. He could make out the titles of his books stacked between the seats, the three-legged metal horse with its Civil War rider and the shellacked horned frog perched on the front dash. Along the ceiling of the car, his pale green topographic maps of Austin with their concentric patterns. Blown-up photos of the three murdered girls, their faces so exaggerated in scale and singularly focused on one element — the convolutions of an ear, a forest of lash reflected in a green iris, a knuckle against the sly corner of a mouth — that they might be mistaken for abstract paintings.

His dazed first thought was that his mother had come for one of her rare visits, her headlights leaping against the back wall of their father's den, and he felt alone and spiteful. He would not go with her, he decided. He would punish her. Every other Saturday, Hollis and his brother, Blake, would call their mother in Corpus Christi on the free long-distance line in his father's downtown feed and grain brokerage firm, their father sitting in his swivel desk chair near the window, looking out at the tops of buildings along Congress Avenue, his face plowing a dark field. Blake, who would always talk first, told their mother how he'd gone over his handlebars on a bike ramp and knocked out a front tooth, and that Peter Parker knew he wasn't a clone because he still loved Gwen Stacy even though she was dead and clones could never feel that kind of love, now, could they? Blake's face shone with a need that made Hollis want to punch him. Their father handed Hollis the phone, and Hollis let the receiver drop and dangle by its cord at his feet. His father's face crumbled like a dirt clod. He could hear their mother's tinny voice down there calling his name. When he finally lifted the receiver to his ear, their mother asked if he'd forgotten about her visit. She exhaled and smoke rose into the ocean-blue sky of an open window somewhere. In his imaginings their mother looked like Gwen Stacy and he dressed her in Gwen Stacy's black hair band, dark top, and purple skirt. The sun was unbearably bright against her bare legs. She pinned the phone between her chin and shoulder and painted her toenails pink, like seashells. Gwen Stacy had their mother's crooked pinkie toes. Her body glistened and made him wince. On the phone, his mother told Hollis she was taking them to Six Flags on Saturday. His mother said, "You remember that crooked house?" She waited for Hollis to remember. "Casa Magnetica," he said, grudgingly. A whole house tilted crazily so that water flowed backwards and oranges rolled uphill. She mentioned a few other exhibits and rides and got the names wrong and he corrected her. She said, "You were always better than me with names." He was quiet.

"We'll have ourselves a time," she said. Then that Saturday, their mother, who was *so, so* very late, stood in the driveway eclipsed in the Monte Carlo's headlights, afraid to turn off the engine because it had died on her so many times on the way. Smoke rose above her head and at first Hollis thought her hair was on fire but then he could smell burnt oil and plastic and their father said, *Carole, we better have a look at that,* but when he opened the hood, fire rose up and burned the hair off his father's forearm. His mother made a low, animal sound deep in her throat and held Hollis and his brother against her, and Hollis wanted to pull away because she smelled different and her breasts were larger and she had colored her hair (*frosted,* she'd said) and he hated his brother, who touched strands of it with a kind of reverence. And the fire melted all the engine wires and blackened the hood, and their mother had to stay two extra days at a motel, where he and Blake swam in the pool and got sunburned and Hollis prayed for the Monte Carlo never to be fixed.

There was a banging on the driver's window. "Mr. Finger?" a man's voice said. Hollis didn't say anything, lying very still under a blanket in the backseat, his body intensely aware of the coarseness of the weave, hoping the voice would just go away. He thought of the boy who'd busted his lip and committed the egregious theft of the conch. And he thought of Truck pulling his brother Trailer alongside Barton Springs Road, and the ways people were linked to one another in time and space by something just outside it, hidden from them always but intuited like the stars in the daytime. Or made into a likeness so that you saw differently. How could he string the everyday beads of his life from this? He didn't know. But the voice outside wanted him to. "I don't have anything you want!" he screamed, and realized it was true but also that he'd never be able to convince them of it. And a terrible light shone down and revealed his nakedness and shame.

10

A YEAR AFTER THE murders, Kate puts the house up for sale. Friends nod sympathetically, say they understand, all those memories. The girls. The marriage to Ray. A few mention different neighborhoods she might consider, a deal on a condo downtown. A new beginning, they say. But, of course, they don't understand. How do you start over with the future gouged out? Margo Farbrother, her friend from the book group, had come by with food all that first week. Margo, with her dark skin like polished wood, high cheekbones. Unlike the others, she didn't veer away from mentioning the girls, asking what the police knew, what they didn't. One night, on the couch, Margo held Kate's head in her lap and stroked her hair with her long fingers. Margo had her own problems. Her stepson, Michael, was in trouble. He'd dropped out of school, gotten arrested for several DWIs, was fucked up on drugs half the time. He and his father, Darnell, fighting constantly. On top of it all, Margo, with endometriosis, suddenly inexplicably pregnant for the first time. She will lose the baby within a month, though nobody knows that now.

On the couch, Kate shook as if she had a fever. Her teeth chattered. Margo seemed to know there was nothing to say. She bent over Kate like a bough, her cheek pressed to Kate's ear. Kate could feel the rise of Margo's belly against her back.

Some mornings Kate stands in front of the bathroom mirror and takes a measure of her body as if for the first time. Her areolas have grown darker with age and remind her of when she was pregnant with the girls. Faint stretch marks still pearl her hips and breasts. The pale fault line of a C-section scar just above her pubic bone, which divides her into before and after.

The Realtor, a squatty salt-and-pepper-haired woman from the suburbs—Kate's consciously avoided the city ones friends recommend; she can't stand the sympathetic stares—comes by the house and, among other things, wants Kate to remove the growing collage of framed photos of the girls from the living room wall. "Everyone wants to imagine their own brood up there," the Realtor says, smiling in a disapproving, hands-on-hips way that reminds Kate of her mother. Kate still expects the Realtor to know their story—as if life didn't go on elsewhere, as if people didn't continue to show up for work, squabble with teenage children, slog through mediocre marriages. For a few seconds they stand in silence in front of the photos. Zadie and Elizabeth in their bikinis at the beach on Galveston Island; Zadie with her first boyfriend, Marcus, at the prom. An empty space next to it where a photo once hung of the girls and Ray, looking sheepish and gangly in his shorts, waving from the deck of his houseboat. Kate removed the photo after she'd found out the detectives had questioned him. He'd grown paler and paler in her mind until he'd become a space on the wall.

"A couple of head-turners," the Realtor says, looking at the photos of the girls. "Who'd want to compete with that?" The Realtor smiles, fiddles with a wall dimmer switch. The Realtor looks out at the living room, says that Kate might want to remove the bead board paneling, go with a neutral color on the walls instead of the sea green, mentions a range of hours they might have showings, dates to host an open house. The ceiling fan makes a *ticka ticka ticka* sound.

Kate readjusts one of the larger studio portraits of the girls from the year before. *Cheesy,* they'd called it. *Staged.* Both their heads tilted awkwardly to one side as if listening to an invisible radio.

The detectives surprised Ray on his houseboat. This was three weeks after the murders, two weeks after Kate had told him to leave. Ray didn't have a phone.

This is how Kate imagines it: Ray, shirtless and barefoot, hobbles to the cabin door on his bad ankles, both of which he shattered falling off the ice cream shop roof while repairing the rain gutters three years before. They ache in the mornings and he has to do exercises to keep them from stiffening up. Because of his ankles, Ray has had to give up his one-weekend-a-month Army Reserve stints in San Antonio. He has a ragged look. Needs a haircut, his beard trimmed, which Kate has done for him for years. Before he opens the door, the urge to talk to Kate seizes him. He wants her there to explain, in her controlled, adult way, to the detectives—one of whom clearly thinks Ray's hiding something by the way he says "discrepancies"—that Ray loved the girls as his own, that he couldn't have ever harmed them, that he wants to kill the men who did, even though he isn't capable of violence, except for the one instance after a friend's wedding reception when he'd drunkenly struck one of the groomsmen after an insult, bloodying his lip.

They take him to the station, put him in a little room with a table and cold plastic chairs. *Can you tell us what happened that night?* the detectives ask again. *When you went by to get the deposit?* There are forty-seven minutes he can't explain. The money was never picked up, the deposit never made. He feels his blood quicken as if he'd risen up out of bed too fast. He's dizzy. His ankles throb. He can still feel the houseboat rocking unsteadily on the water beneath him. He grabs the table leg for ballast. *Oh my sweet Lord,* he says, and puts his hands to his face as if they hold water. There are two things he eventually confesses: first, months before, without Kate's knowledge, he'd raised the value of the fire insurance policies on the ice cream shop. A terrible coincidence, he admits. Terrible. But the building had old wiring, he says; he needed to protect them all from ruin. And two: from time to time—including that night—he'd been fucking Sarah Haven, the insurance agent who sold him the policy.

The Ray in Kate's head will not stop talking. All his words the shapes of things he would have done.

I will go away, Kate thinks. *When the girls finally leave home, I will leave home too.*

11

MICHAEL SOMETIMES REIMAGINES his brother Andrew's last conscious minutes. He conjures up a single, wavering moment among many now inevitable ones that gives Andrew pause. Saves him from bad luck. Instead of coming through the house's side door, where he'll be surprised by the owner, Andrew works his way through the gate and around to the back of the house and hears, through an open window, the murmuring of a baseball game on the radio. The veteran announcer's soothing voice is one Andrew has heard for years. Never impatient or hurried. Even on bad days—a blown save or key dropped ball—there is always some possibility of redemption in it. Andrew, standing there in front of the den window with his duffel bag of tools that says SIMPATICO APPLIANCE REPAIR, can see a fish tank in the corner of the den, its bluish light undulating on the ceiling above. Though there aren't any other lights on in the house and the radio announcer seems to be talking to himself, Andrew thinks: *Not today. This one doesn't feel quite right.* And he makes his way back to his car parked down the street, drives on home, his face intact.

But sometimes it seemed to Michael that it wasn't chance or luck. That there were no decisive moments that could have tipped things one way or another. Sometimes it seemed as if an invisible cord threaded through them all, pulling them along. When he was eleven, his dad showed him a glossy magazine photo of a group of Hindu men on a religious pilgrimage. A dozen hooks pierced the skin of their chests and attached to the hooks were taut colorful ropes being pulled by someone outside the photo. "Whenever you think someone has you by the short hairs, remember this," his dad had said, tapping the photo and laughing. But as a kid, the photo had fascinated and terrified Michael. The men's faces knotted in pain that was also a kind of ecstasy. Their bodies leaning forward, as if into a strong wind.

"But where are they going?" he'd asked his dad.

"Up the mountain," his dad said, leaving it at that.

Later, he'd taken the photo from his dad's dresser and tried to duplicate the hooks and ropes in the bathroom with some safety pins and kite string. But when his chest started bleeding he'd passed out and hit his head on the toilet seat.

Michael was living in an apartment on the east side when the detectives found him, five years after the murders. First, there were the bad portents: the series of odd phone calls with nothing but buzzing on the line, two strange men asking about him at his daughter's preschool, then the carefully handwritten note in green ink under his car wiper blade: *Are you the do-right man?*

He hadn't been hard to find, he supposed, considering the detectives had talked to his wife, Lucinda, who'd abandoned them two months before. For the first month of their trial separation—as Michael still called it—Lucinda would call in the evening and they'd plod through Alice's bedtime routine with exaggerated goodwill. He'd bribed Alice with Reese's Peanut Butter Cups and sodas so she'd speak to Lucinda. Sometimes there would be long silences on the other end and he suspected Lucinda of falling asleep with her mouth open like she did after too much wine. Then something changed. Lucinda's calls took on a manic edge—she phoned at all hours, sometimes claiming he'd stolen Alice from her and threatening to get her back. She said he'd better be careful. She said she had *him* figured out. Michael began to worry about her abducting Alice from school at recess or lunch, and so he sometimes made impromptu visits to the school office around these times—claiming he needed to drop off a jacket or Alice's left-behind chocolate milk—to quiet his anxiety.

A few times on the phone Lucinda had prompted him with people's names, places in Austin where they used to live or hang out years before. She even mentioned the murders, saying she'd seen one of the girls' parents on the news leading up to the fifth anniversary. Something about a memorial fund. "Can you imagine?" Lucinda had said. He asked her why the fuck was she bringing all this up now? Often during these conversations, Alice, as if on cue, would begin calling him from her room: Could he turn the closet light on? Flip her pillow over? Brush her teeth again because she didn't want a gold tooth like his? On the phone, Lucinda would pivot suddenly, confess that she made a mistake, that she missed the old days. She needed Alice back in her life. She was sorry for accusing him of stealing Alice. Sorry for the way she'd acted. She had a sponsor at AA now, she said. He should go too. Then he'd hear her inhale softly—almost mournfully—on her cigarette and could see her lying in some stranger's bed (her sponsor's, probably), the ashtray balanced on her bare belly, the shadowed curve of her breast. He'd say it all would be okay, they'd come through this, if they just learned to trust each other. This was their job now, he said, rebuilding that trust. Part of him actually believed it.

For the past few months, Michael had worked at straddling the gaping hole Lucinda had left in their heads. Sometimes he did this by taking Alice to a kid matinee at the Paramount Theater. Sometimes by picking up Lucinda's slack at the YMCA Preschool parents' day or taking on extra hours working at the men's residence while Alice was there. Sometimes he and Alice would make space ships and submarines from duct tape and discarded boxes they found in the alley behind the apartment. But most of the time Michael spanned Lucinda's absence by levitating on vodka tonics and her left-behind anxiety pills. They'd watch too much bad TV and laugh too loudly and long at his downstairs Korean neighbor's jokes, which Alice didn't understand but laughed at anyway, like the one about a Korean restaurant manager and the missing neighborhood dog.

You seen Fluffy?

You mean that Fluffy with the juicy hind leg? No, I never seen Fluffy.

And Michael opened the back window and he and Alice called and called Fluffy in the alley, and the dog's name came echoing back to them from the mirthless backs of buildings.

Now, in the living room, he watched his unsteady fingers bundle up Alice against the recent cold snap. He struggled a bit with her coat, but she helped one arm through a torn sleeve liner and out the end. He pulled on her wool hat, wrapped her scarf until only her eyes and the bridge of her nose showed. They were partners. She gave him a stoic look over the scarf and he felt the sudden urge to weep. Then he heard an odd clicking sound. He stood perfectly still in the middle of the living room, listening. Alice began to sing a song about the letter H and he shushed her with a finger to his lips. He thought the sound might be coming from the smoke alarm. He tested it and Alice made a cringing face and covered her ears, and he hugged her and told her he was sorry for scaring her. He remembered from somewhere that tapped phone lines made clicking sounds. *Click,* and they'd know all about you and how to separate you from your family. They'd add to some mistake you'd made until you couldn't recognize it anymore. He and Alice stood there taking in the silence of the room. "I'm hot," Alice said from inside her scarf. Then he realized the clicking sound was the grinding of his own teeth.

He pulled on his coat. They held hands down the stairs. Walked up Holly Street through the bright cold to Metz Park, where they liked to play invasion of the zombie dads and prepare a delicate squirrel and tree moss stew. It was late afternoon.

In the park, everything slowed. Stretched out. Light slanted, burnishing the bare branches of pecan trees. They walked past a warped baseball backstop, a paper-strewn dirt field. A trash barrel near the playscape bulged with charred garbage. The whole place smelled like regret.

A few bundled people came and went, their heads swiveling toward the swing sets where Michael was pushing Alice. Michael wondered if he was talking too loud. He was often paralyzed by the thought of some future humiliation gathering just outside his awareness. True, he'd brought much of this on himself, on them—but he was scared of what might happen. Scared of the two men. He tried to remember exactly what he'd told Lucinda about the murders, but it seemed lost among their many quarrels, outrages, and reconciliations. The beginnings of panic fluttered in his chest. But after a while there was only Alice's back and forth arc in the swing. "High, higher, higherest!" Alice yelled. He told her that this was just about as high higher higherest as things could get. She might fall out. And then what?

"Fuck it," Alice said sharply. Michael glanced quickly around to see if anyone had heard her. A woman on a bench was laughing, hand to mouth. She had on sunglasses and a puffy hat that looked like an animal. Her little boy, several years older than Alice, was off climbing the playscape. The woman's good skin and confidence made Michael uneasy. Michael laughed in case that was expected of him, too. Then he said, "Alice," with fatherly disapproval in his voice. He glanced over at the woman. Her sunglasses hid her eyes, but he could feel her scrutiny. He couldn't see Alice's face, only the back of her wool-hatted head as she fell away on the swing and then rose again until she almost touched the low, bare branches hung with fire.

At bedtime, Michael read "Rapunzel" to Alice. His hands were shaking but he hid this by bouncing the book lightly on his thighs. Alice chewed her lower lip thoughtfully. She asked him how he could be sure which things in the story were real and which were made up. He said all of the things in these stories are made up. They couldn't *really* happen. But how did he know? she asked. Well, he said, for instance, even though they might want to, most people don't really hide their children up in towers until they grow up. "That's called child abuse," he said. "People go to jail for that." He smiled. Her face fell a little. She stared off at the darkened window beside them, her own reflection. Alice seemed to consider what it would be like to live at such a height all alone. "In the tower," she said, "you can think about who you're going to be when you grow up and let your hair grow *super* long before they cut it."

12

MOST OF THE evidence that the fire didn't destroy, the water did. Then the short-staffed detectives in Forensics (half of whom were out of town at a conference) botched what was left. The DNA samples were inconclusive. Firefighters and police and EMS paraded through the unsecured crime scene, dragging through sooty water their hoses, klieg lights, and gurneys. Defiling Kate's girls' bodies again and again.

At night, the billboard with the girls' faces—paid for anonymously, Kate discovers—burns bright over the interstate. Elizabeth shaping her mouth into a smile that's a bit sullen, a bit prideful, it's true. Zadie with the pixie cut from her sophomore year Kate had fought against. (*Your beautiful hair is gone* was all Kate could think of to say.) Meredith with her large eyes, her skin darker than Kate remembered.

WHO KILLED THESE GIRLS? the sign says. A reward offered. A tip line number listed.

On the first anniversary, Kate's scheduled to do an interview with a woman reporter from the *Chronicle* but cancels at the last minute, then allows local TV news reporters to trot her out to make her plea. She mentions the hotline number, platitudes about justice and closure. On TV, she's the martyred mother, her face slack with something, though she's not sure yet if it's grief. Watching one of the reports on the ten o'clock news, she is amazed to find she had applied eyeliner and then is angry with herself for caring enough to.

Strangers mail her—in care of the news stations—their children's drawings of her girls in heaven. Heaven has horses. Heaven has tennis and bike riding and seashells by the seashore. In these heavens, there are always the three girls, though it strikes Kate there are times she has almost forgotten about Meredith. Strangers who have lost their children send her recordings—email attachments, CDs—with their survivor stories she'll never listen to. They send their children's school photos, favorite stuffed animals (some tattered, discolored with age), and occasionally even locks of their dead children's hair. These, of course, are meant to bring her closer to the strangers, but they don't.

By the third anniversary, the tip line has conjured eighty-seven confessions. The publicity has brought out all the crazies, Detective Robeson says. He knows only a small number of them hold any promise, so he updates her from time to time so she doesn't go insane. *It was me all along,* they all say. *I was the one.* She asks the detective why they confess. Because, he says, most have nothing else left of value to give.

Kate still suspects everyone. Ray, who, on his knees, begged Kate for forgiveness on the front lawn in front of the neighbors a month after the murders; Bill MacPherson, who delivered the twice-monthly supply of napkins, cups, and bowls to the shop that were

ignited to start the fire, the girls' previous high school band director, who kissed Zadie in the instrument closet when she was in
tenth grade. Even two homeless men, Truck and Trailer, who
shuffled in single-file tandem along Barton Spring Road, so that
one seemed to tow the other. She knows this makes no sense. But
she can't help herself. *The mind reels.* She remembered her mother
saying that. Kate pictured a broken projector spooling film to the
floor. But her mind *did* reel. Flung at her all its confused, spent
images, its nonsense. Spooled out hypotheses until there was
nothing but conspiracy and blame. It's in this way that she contin-
ues to avoid the brutally quiet, small words spoken at her door
that night.

Kate has planned out the whole thing. How when it comes
time, she will write a victim's statement and read it at the trial.
Slowly. To the jury. To her daughters' murderers. Rather than
bear witness to her loss, she will curse the murderers' fathers and
mothers, their wives and children. She will utter heinous prayers.
*May their children plunge out of upper-story windows. May their fathers
be rent limb from limb. May their mothers' eyes be gouged out. May their
penises be severed and inserted into their own gaping mouths.*

She will offer no mercy.
Were her daughters offered mercy?
No understanding.
What was there to understand?
She will bring down their houses.
Then, a few days before the sentencing phase, she'll get one of
the security guards she's been working on during the trial to let
her into the courthouse after hours. She will tell him she left her

cell phone behind. After she recovers the phone from beneath a courtroom seat cushion, she'll ask to use the nearest ladies' room, which is approximately twenty-seven steps and one left turn from the courtroom door. In the restroom's second stall, there's a plumbing access panel just behind the toilet. She knows all about these from the ice cream shop, its bad plumbing. She'll need the Phillips-head screwdriver in her purse to take it off. She'll remove from her purse and place among the pipes the light brown calfskin pouch she's sewn together from the upper portions of the girls' cowgirl boots. It's a bit of a patchwork, it's true. She's hidden the seams as best she can. The raised patterned leather—small spiraling plant shapes, whorls—looks like the topography of a map. The rise and fall of the land. Inside the pouch, a .380 handgun borrowed from her former brother-in-law, the same caliber used to kill her daughters.

Her wrath will be cunning, swift, terrible.

13

NEXT TO HER bed, Rosa keeps a plastic blue crate full of photos, interviews, notes, and news clippings about the murders that tell her nothing. A string of false confessions, some interviews that she'd done early on with Detective Robeson, witnesses in the shop earlier that day. Most remembered nothing except a small fire breaking out near the waffle irons. Later, a few recalled a fight in the parking lot. A disgruntled boyfriend of one of the girls, one said. Skate punks, said another. Homeless guys. Dropouts. The guy with the art car. A young man in a long over-coat. *Squaring the circle,* she thinks, looking at the crate. Where had she heard that?

And now, six weeks before the fifth anniversary of the killings, she has a feature story, possibly even the cover. The city was going to raze the ice cream shop, which had been condemned since the murders. People were angry, unsure of what to do. Until now, except for their yearly plea on the news channels, the girls' families had turned down interviews. Victims' families, Rosa knew, always had their own agendas and timetables. Parents who'd lost children were the most difficult. They went along with interviews to put pressure on the police or potential suspects. Sometimes they wanted to warn others or band them together for a cause, or to simply express their anger at God. Often their grief was complicated by a perplexed sense of failure. *What could we have done differently? If only I'd been there.* Though it was never clear what they might have done to change it. Even years after, the future for many of them—beyond what it might reveal about the past—was a void.

She'd sit with these mothers and fathers on their sofas, framed photos of their children clustered on the coffee table, illustrating what was obvious to everyone but them: that their loved ones never aged. That their children gestated unchanged inside them.

14

I T ' S   A   W E E K before the fifth anniversary of the murders, and a
crowd has gathered in the ice cream shop parking lot, anxious
to get on with things (with what exactly is unclear, even to Kate,
who has helped organize the gathering). The ice cream shop itself
is encircled by a temporary metal fence. Workers have gutted the
building. The smell of diesel exhaust is in the air. A backhoe and a
dump truck idle behind the gate, waiting for the word.

A number of people in the crowd wave photos of the girls, and
signs that read JUSTICE DENIED and NEVER FORGET. Hollis Finger is
among them, his clothes already lightly dusted with crumbled
drywall and ash, the unseasonable heat rising through his shoes
from the asphalt. Television news crews and newspaper reporters
crouch under the pecan trees and sit at the picnic tables in back.
They talk among themselves, unsure what to do. *Is this a protest or
a memorial?* they wonder. Later, under the tree, Rosa Heller, the
reporter, will approach Kate. They'll talk about the tip line, the
donations to the charity that Kate and Meredith's father have
started in the girls' names. Kate will stumble over her words, her
tongue thick in her mouth. *A tribute to their memory,* Kate hears
herself saying. Rosa will remember being startled by pecans
plunking off the picnic table beside them.

The firefighter, Jack Dewey, is there too, near the tree in back. Kate recognizes him from the TV interview of a few nights before: his crew cut, his hands in his jean pockets. *First responder. Discovered the victims. A bare foot sticking out of the water. I have a daughter,* he'd said. He paused and studied the ground. The TV reporter in her red scarf was nodding, encouraging him, wanting desperately to finish his sentences. *I have a daughter,* he said again, *who was lost for a while, who disappeared. But then she came back.* He tried to find the words on the ground. *Not a day goes by,* he said, looking up, *when I don't think of those girls. They are a great comfort.*

Kate thinks she imagined Jack Dewey's last sentence. But she hears it over and over again in her head. *They are a great comfort.*

From where Hollis stands, he can see the shop's flung-open front doors, the yellow police tape still clinging to the glass. A gaping mouth. Every once in a while a helmeted worker emerges from the dark opening, blinking in the sunlight as if waking from a dream.

15

KATE'S HEART SHAPES itself around a lack. A never-will-be. It doesn't grow fonder. It doesn't grow colder. It doesn't forgive. It doesn't even seek to be filled. It only sends itself away and then returns to itself. She doesn't know why. The girls won't tell her yet. So she waits.

In her dream, it's a surprise.

The doorbell rings and rings but it sounds like the buzzer on the dryer. First she thinks it's the newspaper reporter, Rosa, from the anniversary vigil. But it's the girls, home for Christmas, something Kate's forgotten about. She's a bit panicked because the house is a wreck. In fact, it's been recently sold. Boxed up and hauled away by college boys to a new condo downtown, though she knows this happened years ago. How did she forget to tell the girls about the move? she wonders. *Mom? Where are our beds?* She sees their fallen faces in the entryway. They won't even look her in the eye. But they're wearing tank tops, shorts, and flip-flops, their toenails newly painted seashell pink, and they're not at all ready for bed. The resiny sweetness of their sunscreen is in the air. And she knows it's not Christmas at all but the end of summer, Labor Day, the weekend before school starts. They're supposed to be with her in Galveston, at her mother's place. Her memory lapse is unforgivable. In ancient times people used different rooms in their houses, nooks and crannies, even furniture, to store memories so they wouldn't forget. Kate learned this in Latin class. That was how these people memorized speeches. She knew that every ancient woman's bottom dresser drawer held a revolver in a leather pouch, a vibrator, and hair-trigger memories that sprang out when least expected. *Jesus, Mom,* the girls say. *A little too much information.*

They are sitting together, the three of them, on hard plastic chairs in a small room—a room off the kitchen with a tiny window in the door that Kate had somehow forgotten. Inside the room, it smells of men and confused intentions. For some reason Kate can't touch her girls. Then she realizes it's because they are still tender from their sunburns. She hadn't watched out for them, reapplied sunscreen when they went back into the water. This too is unforgivable. She worries that later, without their beds to curl into, they will want to leave.

So when do we meet the new guy? her girls ask. And the waffle cone smell—freed from the small, soon-to-be-forgotten crevices of the house—is so thick that Kate can taste it at the back of her throat.

16

They were daughters.
They were loved.
They were innocent.
They were cursed.
They were unlucky.
They were careless.
They asked for it.
They had no choice.
They were afraid.
They were brave.
They trusted.
They were betrayed.
They suffered.
They heard a voice.
They saw a light.

17

THE WEEK AFTER the ice cream shop demolition, Hollis sees the girls in the bare trees near the Zilker Hillside Theater, drinking peach wine coolers and watching a shabby production of *A Midsummer Night's Dream*. At first, Hollis thinks it's a trick of the moon tower's glow and the shadowy twisting oaks. But then he notices the wind has changed directions and his cedar allergies are coming on and his left ear aches, all of which are signs.

Covered in ash from the demolition, the girls look somehow leaner, taller than they'd been in life. Gone is the baby fat, thick ankles. They hoot from the trees at the Puck, who forgets his lines and whose blocking is so bad that he seems to drift around the stage like an abandoned boat. Elizabeth, a stage manager in high school, takes blocking notes, mimics their stepfather's East Texas drawl: *That there's a piss-poor performance.* From a nearby branch, her sister, Zadie, shakes her head ruefully and speaks out of the side of her mouth: *A sorry-ass sight.* The girls seem to sense Hollis watching them, because they crumble and smoke in the moon-tower twilight. Meredith, her brown skin and dark hair washed out with ash, takes a long swallow from a wine cooler and looks up thoughtfully at the stage. *I like that fella with the horse's head,* she says. They all laugh, because that's Meredith. A horsey girl. Meredith, kicked by a horse when she was ten. Meredith with a curving scar like a bend in a river on her abdomen from the surgery. A kidney lost.

Zadie, in a know-it-all way that seemed to embarrass the others, says, *His name's Bottom and he's got an ass's head. Hello?*

What if we actually were our names? Elizabeth asks.

What do you think, Mare? Zadie whinnies.

Someone is watching us, Elizabeth says.

Meredith holds up an ash-smudged finger like a TV prosecutor. *Or our memories of what we might have been, given a little more time.*

Puck says from the stage that it's just the mushrooms talking.

Actors, Elizabeth says, smirking.

Still, he is kind of cute, Zadie says, feeling wistful.

There is pressure in Hollis's ear. The wind whistles through the bare limbs, stirs the ash. The moon-tower glow weighs down the sky until they are on the bottom of a vast, shallow sea. A sea that's built its monuments of coral and shell and limestone from the death of its own body, from small and terrible sufferings that it's kept hidden from itself.

Oh, it's the art car guy, Meredith says in a way that makes pride and shame flicker through Hollis like heat lightning.

Elizabeth lifts her head and closes her eyes like a medium. *Ah. I see now.*

He's building a monument.

A shrine, Zadie corrects. Holds up an ashy index finger.

A likeness, Meredith says, with a kind of finality.

Hollis can smell their Dolce & Gabbana perfume in the trees now (which they've applied liberally to cover the waffle cone smell) and feels the ache of leaving and coming home (which strikes the girls as funny, since he lives in his car) and remembers suddenly the milky smell of his mother's dress right after she'd had her last child, who was not really his brother, how it thrilled and repulsed him.

He wants to tell them he can't help. That even though they are on the floor of a shallow sea and greatly changed, he can't even tell them what has happened to them or who has done it.

You have carved us on the palm of your hand, they say, one voice handing off to the next like a relay race. And he denies them three times. Until finally they spit him out onto the rocky crags of the park, his ears, two seashells, still murmuring of the sea.

18

THE DETECTIVES TOLD Michael there had been a lucky break in the case. They'd picked him up at the apartment, taken him and Alice to the police station downtown, a squatty low-rise with tall, narrow windows, like coin slots. Michael sat in the detective's hard plastic chairs in a small room with the camera high in the corner. A woman with cropped hair and large eyes had taken Alice from him on the way in. She had an ID tag slung around her neck that seemed to give her the right. Michael told the woman Alice was allergic to strawberries and the woman said she'd make a note about that but then didn't. Michael said for Alice to be good for the nice woman. He'd come get her soon. Alice gave him a look of limitless blame over the woman's shoulder and he'd waved to her until she disappeared through a set of double doors.

There were two detectives. Detective Murrow was fat and kind. Detective Lawrence was sinewy and gruff. They had their parts to play, he had his. That was one of the rules here. They first asked him what he'd been doing in the four years and eight months since the last time Robeson, the lead detective, had questioned him, and his answers seemed, even to him, oddly evasive and incomplete. "When I became a dad, things changed," he said, finally. They tried to scare him with the usual deceptions and wickedness, saying his friends had told them this and that about his whereabouts on the night of the murders. That a witness had finally come forward and placed him in the ice cream shop parking lot late that night. They wondered if Michael might remember any more details to help them out. They had his statement from before, but they were looking for clarity. If he wasn't there, then he needed to tell them where he was. No harm in that, right? Just clarification. Detective Morrow wanted to be his friend. "We know you didn't intend to mislead us, but there are things here, Michael, that just don't add up." Michael tried to steady his Xanax-hands in his lap. What had he intended? Hardly anything he'd ever done.

The detectives knew all about his past: How he'd quit school in the fall, weeks before the murders. He'd been in juvenile detention a couple of times before that. Drug charges. Disorderly. He'd twice been picked up for breaking and entering, though they never caught him with any stolen goods. His dad had hired an attorney to pull his ass out of the fire. They knew quite a bit about his brother Andrew, too. "A cautionary fucking tale," Detective Lawrence said.

"Can I smoke in here?" Michael asked.

Detective Morrow said they'd give him time for that later.

Just like before, Michael told the detectives he would try to help them. But the night is a smear in his mind, he tells them. Indistinct. But he will try to retrace his steps. To get it right. Maybe he saw something? Maybe. He was nearby. He wouldn't deny that. He'd been out with some friends, first over to the Peter Pan Mini Golf, and then drinking beer, he told them, down along the creek like they sometimes did, about eleven. That's when he saw the smoke.

"Right," Detective Morrow said, sitting down heavily in a chair beside him. His midsection fat squeezed into a roll beneath his shirt. "You said that before, Michael. About the smoke. How can you see smoke at night?"

Michael said he didn't know. Maybe he just smelled it, then.

Detective Morrow said, "Now, here's the thing: Your friends have told us you were there, at the ice cream shop."

He saw Lucinda talking and talking with her hands, like she did. The cigarette between her fingers tracing the air. The ashtray balanced on her naked belly. She could go on and on.

Michael wanted to help them, he said. He did. But back then he'd been high or drunk more than half those nights. Could they remember all the things they did when they were seventeen?

"Awful things happened to those girls," Detective Lawrence said with his hard, sinewy face. He tapped a pencil on the table.

"Awful things," Michael said, nodding. Why was he nodding? His skin tightened around his eyes.

"You didn't want those awful things to happen, Michael," his friend Detective Morrow said. "We think someone put you up to robbing the place. But then things went wrong. Things got out of hand." Detective Morrow seemed to drift off momentarily to the place where things always got out of hand and girls never made it back to their beds.

"A clusterfuck," Michael said. The tiny room blurred at the edges, drifted.

"Something like that," Detective Morrow said, nodding.

"Like people just lost their minds," Michael said.

"Some people did," Detective Morrow said. "And some people got trapped."

"What's your daughter's name, Michael?" Detective Lawrence asked.

"Alice."

"Beautiful little girl."

"Thank you."

"How old is Alice? About four?"

Michael nodded. "Am I under arrest?"

"No, sir. You can walk out of here anytime," Detective Lawrence said but didn't mean it.

"Walk right out?" Michael smiled.

"Yes," Detective Morrow said.

"But y'all don't believe me."

"We're not sure what to believe, Michael."

"Believe I was never there," Michael said, like an incantation.

Something elusive was happening in the room. Above them, one of the fluorescent lights flickered and buzzed. Standing at the front of the table, Detective Lawrence shifted on his feet like an athlete. Detective Morrow sat back in his chair with his arms crossed, legs splayed. The door between them was a narrow slab of beige. Framed for a moment in the door's small window, the face of the woman with the large eyes who'd taken Alice from him.

Detective Lawrence sighed the way he did before he threw something or ruffled his papers or walked behind you so you couldn't see what he was up to. He blurred a little around the head and shoulders.

How long would this go on? What could he say to make it end? He looked toward the small window again and Andrew's face looked back.

Michael's bowels filled with sand.

"Michael? You okay?" Detective Morrow asked.

Michael nodded, unconvincingly.

"Let's back up a bit. Who was there that night? Down by the creek with you?"

"Just friends, you know. Scott Carl, probably. A girl named Letty I used to hang out with."

"Anybody else?"

"That's all I can remember."

"What if I told you they never saw you down by the creek?" Detective Morrow said. "Would that surprise you?"

He tried to imagine what might surprise him but came up empty. His jaw ached. He thought he could hear Alice calling him from some other room.

"We know you were there, Michael," Detective Morrow said. "Who else was there?"

"I'd really like to help y'all," he said, weakly. He was grinding his teeth again. He needed a cigarette.

"We know there were two other men. We know you didn't mean for this to happen."

"I saw him just sitting there on that picnic table," Michael said. "He didn't say much. Didn't tell me which way to go, what to do, or anything like that. He was never good at that kind of stuff."

"Who are we talking about here?" Detective Morrow said.

"Andrew busted my nose once. I had to go to the hospital."

"Stay with me, Michael."

"He didn't mean to. It just happened."

"Like with the girls?" Detective Morrow said.

"They weren't supposed to be there," Michael said.

"I believe you," Detective Morrow said.

"So why were they there?" Michael asked. He knew something significant pivoted off the answer to this question. In one version of the night in his head, he hears the girls' singsong voices in the parking lot, the jangle of car keys as the car starts, the first guitar chords of a song on the radio.

"I don't know," Detective Morrow said. "Who else was there who wasn't supposed to be, Michael?"

Everything Detective Morrow didn't know made Michael want to weep. His ignorance was unbearably large.

Michael watched the patterns of light on the white table, a trapezoid, rectangle. *No names,* the younger man had said. Whatever you put a name to would lose its power. It was the opposite of what most people thought, the younger man said. Sometimes not knowing was stronger than knowing. The older man Michael hated said that if that was true, then Michael was the strongest of all. The older man grinned. Michael thought it was all bullshit but he liked hearing the younger man talk, the cadence of his voice. *Inviolable* was a word the younger man used. Their bond was inviolable. Michael would regret it terribly if he even thought of breaking it. *What are men,* the younger man said, *without their word?*

"He has a real way with people," Michael told Detective Morrow. "He could smile and get you to do just about anything."

"Whose smile, Michael?" Detective Morrow asked. He put a hand on Michael's shoulder. The detective looked at him as if he understood the struggles of someone who worked with his hands for a living, someone with responsibilities, a father, like the detective himself, who wanted to do the right thing but for some reason never could. Michael knew if he laid down his burden, the detective would carry it. And for a moment Detective Morrow's bulk seemed to fill the whole room and Michael felt weightless, hardly anchored to the earth at all.

19

J ACK LOST HIS daughter, Sam, at the River Festival when she was six. His friends said what happened was understandable, considering his wife's aneurysm, her lengthy hospitalization. All the stress. But he knew they were lying. It happened because he was selfish. Thinking about his dick. He'd been standing at a raffle booth near the Ferris wheel, talking with Carla Looper, who had taught school with his wife. He'd always found Carla attractive and after a few beers he'd gotten the courage to talk to her. It would be a few years before they slept together, a half dozen more before Carla moved in with him and Sam. Sam, six years old, was twenty feet away, watching people throwing baseballs at the dunking booth. She made an exaggerated pitching motion toward him and smiled—she often pretended to like baseball for his sake. Carla counted out her register and asked him how Sam was dealing with her mother's absence. Jack told her that Sam would sometimes sit with her mother in her hospital room among the whirring machines and tell her old jokes, ones they'd enjoyed together before the aneurysm. *Time flies like an arrow. Fruit flies like a banana.* Carla smiled, her face open and sympathetic. And for a moment—and this is something Jack's nearly forgotten—he had pictured a naked Carla, moving her hips on top of him, her face lit with pleasure. He'd tried to push the image away. Then he'd glanced over at the dunking booth cage and Sam had vanished.

The River Festival director made the announcements over the loudspeaker. For a moment, there was a deflated silence in the crowd and the parents seemed to glance around for their children, touch them on shoulder or head to confirm that they were real. Volunteers with flashlights combed the dusky grounds and the park beyond. Wading into the duckweed and cattails and calling for Sam along the shore, the mud sucking at his tennis shoes, Jack could see families canoeing nearby, their faces appearing here and there in the glow of flashlights. Their calm voices traveled over the water. He could hear paddles strike the surface. A female voice somewhere said that the river was an ancient seabed once. An estuary. They seemed to take part in another world.

Jack took deep breaths, shoved aside terrible images that strobed his mind, focused on his search-and-rescue training. He organized parents and some of the off-duty police who were working security at the festival. They made a makeshift grid and walked it, their flashlights flaring off parking lots and the Zilker Hillside Theater stage, where they'd just held a summer-stock play. People were still scattered here and there on blankets, drinking, talking, under the false glow of the moon tower. Sam's name echoed from the tree-lined edges of the park.

The year before, he'd taken Sam and his wife to a spot below the Springs for a swim. This was two months before the aneurysm, before things changed so abruptly. It was just before sunset and they'd looked up from the edge of the water to see a plume of smoke and fire trailing high over their heads. A flock of grackles wheeled crazily over the water and up the banks of the creek. He remembered standing knee-deep in the current with his family, looking up at the smoldering sky, thinking it portended something. But it wasn't clear what.

"Oh, it's the space shuttle," his wife said, suddenly, "coming back to Earth."

"Why is it on fire?" Sam said.

"It only looks that way," Jack said.

"Like in a movie," Sam said matter-of-factly, staring up at the plume.

"The astronauts are safe and sound inside," his wife said. "They're looking out the windows."

"Can they see us?" Sam asked.

"We're too tiny," Jack said.

"Are we like microbes?" Sam asked.

"They probably see rivers and hills," his wife said.

"What about our house?" Sam asked.

"I don't know. They're pretty far up there," Jack said.

"When you're that far up, the ground misses you more."

"Maybe so," Jack said.

The grackles wheeled and cried out like rusty gates. The sky burned.

Jack's wife turned to him, smiled. "I'm glad I'm here with you and Sam to see this," she said. "It's really something."

The morning Jack's wife was struck down by the aneurysm, she'd done something they could never explain: she'd taken a baseball bat from the hall closet and shattered the three bay windows in the den.

Two park employees found Sam near the canoe rental. In the car on the way home, Jack had asked Sam why she'd wandered away, how she'd vanished. His blood pressure was up. There was a steady pain behind his eyes. Sam said she'd made herself invisible. It wasn't hard, she said. It's like how in a joke one word can hide behind the meaning of another. It's right in front of you but you don't see it. *Invisible.* She said she didn't realize she'd gone so far until she saw the rental canoes yoked together with a chain, paddles sticking from the barrels, the blue light at the end of the dock. She said she'd walked there with a boy. "What boy?" he'd asked. She said, "The one who teaches you how to be invisible."

20

WHAT HOLLIS REMEMBERS: He was driving a medical supply truck at night along the rutted dirt road to Mosul, something he'd done dozens of times. A companion beside him was singing or humming a song Hollis couldn't name but that the companion had sung or hummed before. A dust storm had just passed through the Iraqi village they were entering, and Hollis could taste grit in the air. Dust swirled in the headlights and it seemed for a moment like they were driving on the bottom of a silty sea. Then came the bright flash of light. Hollis remembers thinking that the light was both terrible and beautiful and that if circumstances were different he would have looked at it longer. It lit up the road and surrounding desert and revealed what he never noticed anymore—a half-eaten dog carcass, an old tire, a woman's discarded purple slipper—but it seemed to flash inside him, too, and he imagined in that instant that all his organs were distinct and visible, which he thought was funny because as a medic he knew organs were often unrecognizable when looked at on the inside. Like one organism, indivisible.

There was no bomb concussion. Instead, a girl child appeared in the road. She wore a blue flowered dress. Her face was calm. Hollis swerved. The truck went into the ditch.

The roaring of the Lord was deafening. But it was hard to tell what it all meant.

After the truck flipped over, he decided to lie there for a bit before trying to open his eyes. Get his bearings. He couldn't lift his head but somehow knew his skull was pointed to the east, toward Mecca. The air had a burned smell. Also blood. Shit. His singing or humming companion's twisted body was somewhere around. He tried to plan triage in his head. He couldn't hear a thing except for a singsong call to prayer, which also sounded like the music to an old TV variety show being played underwater. The image of the girl in the road lingered behind his eyelids. Fired his brain by some alchemical process. He wondered if he was bleeding from his ears. To take his mind off this, he took an inventory with his hands, opened his jacket, felt along his chest, rib cage, abdomen. He seemed to be dressed in a suit of chain mail. He remembered thinking, lying there in the darkness waiting on the assassins, about a TV documentary he'd once seen about ancient cave paintings in France. The absolute darkness of the caves, the effete guide said, was essential to the painters. The void was what made it possible to see things as if for the first time. The guide demonstrated with his girlish hands how these painters—after receiving their visions in that dark—used firelight and shadow and the pitted and swollen cave wall itself to animate their work in space and time. How the painters made horses and bison leap just as they did in the mind of God.

21

WHEN THE YOUNGEST of us slept with Marcus Bell, we pretended she hadn't. Marcus Bell, who mowed yards all summer and whose sweat smelled like fresh-cut grass. Marcus Bell, who had a collection of creepy baseball player bobbleheads on a shelf above his bed, and dark red areolas like pepperoni slices. Marcus, off-limits because the oldest of us had gone out with him. The youngest of us never told about Marcus because it would've changed everything, even though that's why she did it: to change everything. But the change that it brought surprised her. Something about Marcus moving inside her on his lumpy bed made her think of a boat lost in a vast sea. She buoyed him up. He was just a small thing, hardly there at all. She rolled on and on. Filled up with only herself. It was a lonely feeling. She wondered if to Marcus it seemed like he was lost in a sea of grass, like an unending prairie. She tried to explain this lonely feeling to him when he drove her home afterward, but grass clippings had filled his ears and he grew nervous and stared straight ahead at the road and said something about how pretty she was and how he hoped they could have more special times. But she knew they would go on just like before, in ignorance of each other, and she would see him at Mangia Pizza that next week and he would stop by our table and smile the way he did and ask if he could have her pepperoncini and one of the boys with him would laugh. But she would see in Marcus's eyes that part of him knew he was a boat lost in a vast sea.

So we pretended about Marcus because if the others of us knew, the youngest of us wouldn't be allowed to go riding anymore with the horsey girl or be invited along to scavenge for theater costumes at thrift stores. But of course we knew. Knew from the smallest things. The way she stopped wearing so much makeup (except a little base and powder to hide the hickeys Marcus had given her). The way she hugged the others of us for no reason. The way she absently cocked her head and listened to the vast sea inside herself.

See how we are? We know and don't know.

I just wish I had more memories, one of our mothers says from somewhere, and we know we are near our anniversary. Jesus H. Christ, we think, because we know what's coming. Suddenly one of us has her pixie haircut from sophomore year. Another of us wears the round glasses that made her face look fat before she got contacts. The youngest of us feels her retainer push against the roof of her mouth and can't help but lisp.

I can still smell their hair after a bath.

We suspect she's doing laundry, because that's when these thoughts often come, while matching socks. Laundry is dangerous that way.

They are a great comfort, the firefighter said.

Then we see one of our mothers on the laundry room floor, hands bound with a bra, mouth harnessed with a ligature made from panties. We're afraid. *Don't leave us like this,* we say (the retainer gets in the way, so it sounds lispy and far off).

The firefighter knows something, one of our mothers says through the ligature.

He just might, we say. *The new guy always seems to.*

Maybe I'm imagining it.

Even so, we say. *The plot thickens. We go forward rather than back.*

Maybe I'm going crazy.

Her cheek against the floor tile, one of our mothers is conscious of her heart beating. How it sends itself away and returns to itself.

We've been there, we say.

She watches the clothes tumble in the dryer window and thinks of tiny particles falling through an endless void and how by chance a few collide with others. How all the stars, planets, animals, and people came to exist by collisions like this and will one day fizzle out into nothing. But in the meantime the particles keep going. Maybe sadder and wiser, but they mosey on (okay, our words, not hers), colliding here and there, a part of us remaining a part of them. And though the physics of all this is over our heads, we're suddenly there under the utility cabinets in the fluorescent light that's always on the fritz. Our mother matches socks in her head on the floor and thinks for a moment she can smell our perfume but decides it's just the fabric softener. She stares into the flickering light for a moment, narrows the gap. *See?* we say. *See how small a thing it is that keeps us apart?*

22

YEARS BEFORE, WHEN Rosa moved from Chicago to Austin, her boyfriend, David, had followed her. At the time, it seemed like a good fit. She'd take journalism classes and work for the university paper, he'd play in bands, do his music writing. David was obsessed with early-twentieth-century blues and jazz, the musicians from that era who seemed to have disappeared without a trace. Ciphers, he called them. He'd talk excitedly about how these anonymous people had invented modern music out of thin air. How they'd made a place for themselves in the future while their own time passed them by. "Sort of like you," she'd said to him once over breakfast, and he smiled in a funny way that made her think for some reason of the surf sucking sand from beneath her feet.

David played guitar, trumpet, and clarinet in a band that sounded like a drunken carnival. The band's songs were filled with dark longings and melodrama. People went crazy from rejection and loneliness. They leaped out of church choir balconies or came too close to a space heater in their gauzy nightgowns. The innocent died while the guilty went on. The band's lead singer maniacally beat a big bass drum at the front of the stage. The audience sang along drunkenly. For months, Rosa had a crush on the singer, particularly his mouth, then briefly on the singer's pale girlfriend, who dressed like Fay Wray. For the first eight months she spent Friday and Saturday nights at Liberty Lunch or the Hole in the Wall. She would sometimes have to drive to Melody Mart for new clarinet reeds or to retrieve a pickup amp for David. A gofer. She didn't mind.

By that first spring, Rosa had her own opinion column in the university paper and a reputation as a first-rate editor. She won a prize for a five-part series she'd written on sexual violence for which she'd interviewed dozens of people—professors, students, janitors, librarians, police, administrators. She stayed late at the paper, smoked more than ever, drank after deadlines with her coworkers, and either came late or didn't make it to David's shows. David became sullen and paranoid. He complained about the heat. His prospects. Fire ants. Her fluctuating weight—her quitting cigarettes for a time didn't help. He lost interest in his 78 record collection, which she'd helped haul down from Chicago, records he used to transcribe old song lyrics for archivists. He seemed to resent her recent success, resented that his gigs had dried up in the early nineties recession and that the bands he played in weren't serious enough or authentic enough. He threatened to legally change his name to Jelly Roll Morton until she told him it would invalidate the apartment lease. A little later, he threatened the drunken carnival band's lead singer with his drum mallet, as if imitating one of their songs. He got voted out of one band, then another. He and Rosa fought over rent money and utilities. And, of course, they had less and less sex. The last few times they did, he'd insisted on entering her from behind, which she'd always liked but now found unsettling. Something about his breathing had changed, she thought. He had the dry, metallic smell of their old radiator in Chicago. So she began putting him off, finding reasons to stay away until he was asleep. Planning a way out.

One night, she came home late and the lights were off and David was sitting in the living room listening to gypsy jazz. Beer bottles cluttered the glass coffee table. He'd asked her absently about the newspaper and she told him about recent goings-on. Gossip. Told him a funny story about Graham, the managing editor.

They sat there in the near dark and she took off her shoes, rubbed her feet.

He smiled at her in a way that said he'd been into the medicine cabinet. He made a strange little chuckle in his throat. "Are you fucking him? That Greg or whoever?"

"Do you think that's funny?"

"No. Not very." He looked out the window with a stricken face, as if he saw this Greg slinking along the fence line. "You just seem to talk about him a lot."

"Graham has chronic psoriasis." She stared at him.

David downed his beer, opened another. Lit a cigarette.

"Can we turn on some lights in here?" she said.

Django Reinhardt's "Summertime" came on. David told her that Django Reinhardt started out a decent guitarist but not a great one. The best and worst thing that ever happened to him, David said, was that one night after a show, on the way to bed, he knocked a candle over in his gypsy caravan home that he and his wife, Florine, shared. Florine had beautiful long dark hair. Turned out, David said, the candle set fire to piles of little celluloid flowers Florine made to supplement their measly income.

"Ah, a musician's life," Rosa said.

David looked at her. Smiled his medicine-cabinet smile.

The next-door neighbors' dogs started barking along the back fence.

Anyway, David said, Django's nightshirt caught fire. Florine tried to smother it with a blanket, but her long hair went up in flames too. Django eventually smothered the flames, dragged her outside, but it was too late, David said. Django was devastated. His wife lost. His fret hand and a leg severely burned. Scar tissue formed on the hand until it resembled something like a claw. Essentially he had to relearn to play the guitar from scratch, David said. He paused and listened intently to Django Reinhardt's strumming. "Two functional fingers on his fretting hand," David said. "Two!"

They sat there in the buzzing silence after the song. David fidgeted, took a drag off his cigarette. Leaned over and moved the needle on the record. A jangly, fast-tempo song began to play.

> *Someday, when you grow lonely*
> *Your heart will break like mine and you'll want me only*
> *After you've gone away...*

Rosa felt dizzy. Red celluloid flowers bunched in her head. The room smelled like burning hair. She got up and started for the bathroom, but David stood up and blocked her way. She tried to maneuver around him but her movements seemed slow and clumsy and she wondered for a moment if she was asleep. David grabbed her hand, gripped her hard around the waist and attempted to dance her around the room, to heave her roughly over boxes of books and stacks of 78s. Empty beer bottles clattered to the floor.

"You're hurting me," she said, pulling away.

"We're dancing," David said, smiling, his eyes jittery in his head. He tried to grab her hand but she pulled away from him, moved toward the back door. He swung his arm out and hit her in the side of the head with the flat of his palm. Everything grew bright and hot. There was a ringing in her ears. In front of her, his face a knot of hatred and contrition. He said he was sorry, that it was an accident. He tried to take her in his arms. Rosa shoved him and he stumbled back, catching his heel on a box of 78s. His body seemed to pause in the air for a moment before he fell and shattered the glass tabletop.

23

FROM THE SIXTH floor of the police station, Michael could see the cars and trucks passing along the interstate below. He followed a northbound red Boar's Head truck until it rose onto the upper ramp, where it would pass beneath a billboard with the girls' faces. He never drove north along the interstate and had nearly forgotten why. He never went to Juan in a Million anymore for breakfast because he thought he'd seen the older man eating migas there once. He never told anyone about the camera or tripod lighting or DVDs he'd found in the back of the Volvo. *Oh, that,* the younger man had said, later, as they drove over to the ice cream shop, as if he'd been meaning to mention it all along. *What good is a fire insurance policy without documentation?* The younger man smiled in a way that made Michael think of someone leaning in for a kiss. Outside, purpled lawns and houses drifted past. Michael remembered an erection swelling in his jeans and the sudden urge to leap out of the car.

He would have left town already with Alice if it hadn't been for the recent court visitation order Lucinda had filed through an attorney—a ploy of some kind, he supposed, to eventually get money out of him or maybe out of his dad. How had things gotten so out of hand?

Outside the jail, Michael carried Alice across the intersection at Seventh Street and then under the interstate. Eighteen-wheelers roared overhead. The smell of exhaust made him nauseous. He asked if Alice was hungry and she said the nice lady gave her a Happy Meal and a vanilla milkshake. She was tired and dreamy-eyed now and only wanted to be carried. As they passed under the interstate, Michael thought he saw one of the plainclothes detectives who'd picked them up earlier parked in a white Mercury. They'd want to talk to him again tomorrow, to clear up a few things, Detective Morrow had said. Maybe they'd need to take a drive over near where the ice cream shop used to be. But he wasn't under arrest, no. There was no need for that. They were just talking. Michael could still feel the weight of Detective Morrow's hand on his shoulder.

He went through a mental list of all the things he and Alice would need, but it seemed to run on and on like water from a tap. Alice asked to ride on his shoulders, so he raised her up over his head. The wind was blowing from the south now, and the late-afternoon sun warmed his back. He felt oddly at ease for a moment—as if for once his options were clear. As if every moment now had a cellophane sheen that he might poke through to what was really happening.

Alice said, "Look at the shadow on the ground, Daddy. We're a giant."

On the other side of the interstate, he flagged down one of the cabs driving by, which he knew rarely stopped near the police station. The cabdriver looked him over, as if debating whether criminals gave kids rides on their shoulders. Michael glanced back at the detective in the white Mercury and then helped Alice into the cab. The wind kicked up, swirling dust and sand, and Michael stumbled into the backseat, nearly blinded.

Michael was twelve, Andrew fifteen.

Their mom taught English at the community college. Student essays were always piled on her desk in the den. She called the students her other babies. Freaks, Andrew and Michael said. Towelheads. Jasbeer Mowat was one. "You want mo wat?" Michael kept saying until their mom got mad. "These folks haven't been given everything like you two," she'd snapped. Once in a while she would read a good essay to them. A fifty-year-old woman wrote about going to the doctor for some tests and finding out she had a tumor the size of a cantaloupe in her uterus. Afterward, the woman went home and prepared her husband and kids for the worst. But when she went back for more tests, they found out the tumor was a baby instead. "What kind of idiot doesn't know they're pregnant?" Andrew had said, grinning at Michael. She'd tossed the essay down, glared at him, said he'd missed the point, and besides, what did he know, had he ever been pregnant?

But the best essay Michael stole. He stashed it in the air vent beside his bed. He took some shitty ones too, so it wouldn't look suspicious. Their mom pulled her hair out looking for them. One night, after he'd gotten back from smoking weed and watching Comedy Central at a friend's house, he'd gone straight to his room, pulled the essay from the vent, and held it under the lamp, its edges brown-smudged from his fingers.

Videsh Deshmuke
English 1310
Personal Narrative
Prof. Kay Greer

Delta Crash

My wife Madya and I were returning from my father's burial ceremony in India. On the plane, I was thinking of how the last meal I prepared for my father—Emperor's Saffron Chicken—was not up to his standards. "A little dry for me," the old bastard said. "And the chutney too lemony." To think how this bothered me then. I wanted so badly to make up to the dead.

On the plane, I remember my wife's head turned toward the window. She was suffering from homesickness already. Her short, modern hair and capped teeth made everyone in my family look a second time. Is this you after all, Madya? their glances said. She did not fit anymore. And because of this, we grieved together. I for my father, she for her old life. It was not that she hated our new life, the life of the Indian restaurant we ran together. It was that she could never taste the other life in the same way.

The night after my father's burial, I lay on the bed in the dark, weeping. She came and sat beside me and ran her fingernails through my hair for a very long time. She sang a song to me in Hindi. Her skin smelled of tea leaves.

On our flight back to Dallas, I remember the many swimming pools below, winking in the sun. Then the plane dropped beneath us, too sudden. Madya grabbed my hand.

The oxygen masks fell from the ceiling. There was an explosion. Blue flame rolled down the aisle, like some child's enormous lost ball. Then the world was torn in two.

I was strapped in my seat, sitting in a great field. Sirens were screaming. In my nose, the odor of fuel and something I could not name. Clothing was scattered on the ground. Above, I saw blue sky, darkness, blue sky again. Smoke was coming from a dark, crushed shape in the distance. I felt its heat. I knew the shape was part of our plane. Impossible thoughts whirled in my head. I was outside what a moment before I had been inside. My eyes closed. I still felt Madya's hand in mine. Then I saw my father across the field, hobbling on his bad ankles. He was wearing his white chef's smock and hat. He came to me. "You are certainly lucky," he said in Hindi, patting my shoulder. "A big bird crashes like that and you end up sitting here as though you were watching a movie."

"Father, is Madya still holding my hand?" I asked. He did not answer. He then told me a story. One evening he was cooking at the restaurant and stepped into the dining room. He saw the customers eating his chicken kabobs and curried lamb. He felt satisfied. Then it occurred to him that just as he had prepared their food, they, in turn, were being prepared for Shiva's terrible appetite. That one day Shiva would lift them up, eat them like nan.

"Is Madya holding my hand?" I asked again.

"We worry over each other, the living and the dead," my father said, looking thoughtful.

"It is not enough. I need her hand," I said.

My father shook his head and told me I was still angry over his criticism of my Emperor's Saffron Chicken.

I remember a baby crying in the distance. At some point, my father hobbled away, and the paramedics found me in the smoke. And, of course, they found Madya's body soon after, in another part of the field. Six months ago, a newspaper reporter came by the restaurant. He ordered tandoori-style shrimp. He asked me how my life had changed since the time of the crash, seven years ago. Had I come to terms with my loss? I thought about this. I watched him eat. I remembered Madya running her fingernails through my hair that time, our joined grief. "I am always coming to terms," I said, finally. "It does not end."

Michael's head hummed. He put the essay down, and for a minute he saw Videsh in the smoky field with his dad. What they were talking about was important. But he couldn't hear what they were saying because that baby was crying so loud. Then he wondered if Videsh and Madya had a kid somewhere. He thought how babies, before they're born, can hear their parents' voices outside. But words don't go with anything in that dark.

He got up, put the essay back. He turned off the lamp and lay down.

Outside, the sprinkler system turned on. *Chit, Chit, Chit,* it said.

24

Last year Kate had made a New Year's resolution to get out more. To meet new people, reconnect with her old friends. But it didn't happen. So on the heels of the fifth anniversary, she'd RSVP'd to an early-December Christmas party some of her old neighbors were having. She felt a little raw so soon after, a little disloyal somehow. Her dreams still gave her pause — the girls' quarrelsome visits, the odd new rooms added to the existing ones, the disquieting presence of men. She'd been preoccupied with the approach of the anniversary but now needed to get back to running her three miles along the river, eating better. She wasn't thirty-five anymore but she still had her looks, hadn't let herself go. She'd even called up Margo Farbrother, who was pregnant for a second time. Margo who'd intimidated her early on with her good skin, high cheekbones, and shapely ass. Margo had convinced her to rejoin the book group. They were reading *Moby-Dick* now, Margo said, but skipping all the whale stuff. "Where are all the women?" Margo had said. "How about throwing us a bone?" There were more troubles with Margo's stepson. Calls from his probation officer. Why had she and Darnell thought having a kid would change Michael? Margo wondered. He's adrift, she said, a lot like his brother Andrew, according to Darnell. Margo worried about Michael's daughter, Alice, too. What might be in store for her if things broke a certain way? Michael seemed oblivious. "It's like that old joke," Margo said. "Why should I care about posterity? What's posterity ever done for me?" She laughed nervously.

"You'll have your own kiddo to worry about soon enough," Kate said. "You'll be such a great mom." Kate was a good listener. It felt liberating to be out of her own head. To worry about someone else.

"Wow. It just never ends, this worry stuff," Margo said, and then there was a silence on the phone.

"It's fine," Kate said. "It's fine. And you're right."

It was late when Kate showed up at the Christmas party. She'd even brought a date: Edward. She'd met him online. He worked contracts in the legal department at Dell. Edward had large hands and he bit his nails. But they were clean nails, she reminded herself. She ignored his bitterness about his divorce, concentrated on his attentiveness to her, their mutual interest in hiking and bird-watching—something, along with the book group, that she'd picked back up. Edward sometimes made birdlike sounds in his sleep, odd little clicks and coos. The sex wasn't bad. Edward joked that he'd gotten such a late start because his strict Southern Baptist family viewed sex as an awful, filthy act that should only be saved for someone you marry.

Kate downed a half bottle of wine before Edward picked her up.

At the party, she saw her old neighbors. Christine Fountain, who'd helped her plant a garden the year after the girls died—the zucchini squash they'd planted had taken over half the yard. Christine, picking purple hull peas and bringing them into Kate's kitchen to shell. Christine, with her deeply tanned arms, who rode her bike everywhere in the heat. Winnie Lipsy, a nurse in the neonatal wing at the hospital where the girls were born and whose reserve reminded Kate of her mother. Kind eyes, she thought. The Gilmores with their two sons, toddlers when she'd moved. Jennifer, their mom, had let herself go, she thought. Jowly. Saggy ass. Then Kate felt ashamed for thinking it. Jennifer's boys raced through the long dining room, bumped into Kate, spilling some of her wine on Edward, then slid on the wood floor and tumbled noisily into the den. Jennifer apologized, wiped at the spot on Edward's sweater. Edward smiled weakly, said no problem, that he'd be sure to clothesline the boys the next time through. Edward swung his arm out. "Whack," he said. Kate laughed, said Edward had been raised by wolves. Jennifer looked at them both blankly. Edward was hard to read. His deadpan sense of humor. But she liked him for it. He was who he was. Who was she?

Many of the people at the party had called to check in on her at various points over the years. They were decent and kind. Why had she ever moved? she wondered. Kate had the disquieting feeling that of all the people in the room, she had changed the least. Edward poured her another glass of white wine in the kitchen and she pulled on her sweater and followed him out onto the deck. The moon hung just over the tree line beyond the fence. A knot of people, some of whom she recognized, had gathered on the deck to smoke. A tennis-playing friend of Ray's said a shy hello. Claire, a woman she used to carpool with when the girls were in grade school, saw her and came over to talk. They kept it light, talked about all the changes to the neighborhood, the spike in property values. At the edge of the deck, a man with a crew cut was drinking a beer and talking with Brent Gilmore, who wore a hat with reindeer antlers. The man seemed familiar, even the way he stood, his feet splayed, a hand jammed in his jeans pocket. A much younger woman, a girl, really, with long braided hair joined him, grabbed his forearm. The young woman caught Kate staring and Kate looked away.

Wine hummed in her head. Her mouth was dry. She looked around for Edward for some kind of ballast.

A string of firecrackers went off in the distance. In the middle of the yard, a group of teenage boys was hunched over a large clear plastic bag. One of the boys held a lighter inside the bag and lit candles sticking from a block of Styrofoam. "Better water down your roofs!" one of the men shouted from the porch, and everyone laughed. The fire balloon threw shadows across the yard, made spindly human figures against the fence. After a few minutes, the balloon swelled with hot air, rose slowly above the yard. A kind of quiet fell over the crowd as they watched. For a moment, to Kate, their upturned faces seemed to betray fretful memories, all their regrets. She wondered what her own face looked like.

The fire balloon floated over the creek bed behind the house. Illuminated live oak branches and telephone wires, where tennis shoes hung by their laces. She could see Edward standing on the lower rungs of the fence, watching. A few people who'd just come out onto the porch whooped and hollered drunkenly. The teenage boys, sheepish and amazed, stood around in the yard with their hands in their pockets, with no plan for what came next.

Kate's head detached from her body, drifted upward.

"Ms. Ulrich?" a man's voice said, and Kate turned. The man with the crew cut stared back. The young woman stood behind him, smiling but appraising Kate all the same. The girl and the man had the same thick dark eyebrows, brown eyes. And it was only then that Kate remembered his halting interview with the TV news reporter and knew who he was.

25

ON HER COMMUTE, Rosa sometimes listens to old taped interviews she did for pieces she never wrote. Voices of ex-cops, witnesses, medical examiners, victims' families, neighbors. Labeled and put away for some future use. Stories that have grown more inscrutable over time. More like intimations.

Here's something that might interest you. There was this guy who'd race his old Firebird through my neighborhood. This is the way he walked his dogs. I shit you not. The dogs would run through the yards chasing the Firebird. He'd roll right through stop signs. My kids were young then and always riding their bikes around, so I'd yell at the guy from my porch. Other neighbors did too, but they were wary of him, you could tell. You could see him hunched behind the wheel in there. He stared straight ahead, paid no attention. The kids in the neighborhood made up stories about him like kids do. He'd poisoned his children but got off on a technicality. He tortured runaways in his basement and fed them to his dogs. Urban myth stuff. Anyway, after a couple of these incidents I decide to go visit his place, three or four blocks away from my house. I wasn't sure what I'd say exactly but I was going to make an impression. So I get over there and he's got all these antique carnival arcade games on his porch. He fixed them up, sold them on eBay, I suspect. Morgana the Fortune Teller was one, I remember — the upper torso of a woman in a red velvet-lined box. Anyway, I know the guy is home because I can hear the TV going. When I knock, dogs start barking inside. A whole pack, by the sound of it. He comes to the door. Hobbles a bit, like he's got a bad knee. He's disheveled. Dark circles under his eyes. Nervous. He has a long screwdriver in his hand. The dogs keep barking. It's loud. He keeps turning back to them, talking in a language I can't follow. I think about him running the stop sign, smashing my son's bike, launching him in the air. And for some reason, I don't know why, I introduce myself as someone I'm not. I tell him I'm from Austin Animal Control. I'm coming from work, in a jacket and tie, so I look semi-official. I tell him that there have been complaints about the number of dogs he keeps in his house, about the dogs being a danger to the community. I tell him the dogs may have to be removed. Euthanized. He looks at me like he's examining a piece of food that might've gone bad. His eyes jitter around as if he's mulling over his options. I'm watching the screwdriver out of the corner of my eye. Then he says, in English, without raising his voice, that he'd like to come to some agreement. There is no need for this, he says. He glances back inside the house, and his face stiffens, like he's imagined suddenly what all this might mean. He seems spooked. I notice the close smell of the house now, the dog smell, but something behind that, something that made me think of dirt and roots. Or maybe that's just in retrospect? Who knows? Anyway, the dogs are really going at it now. So I tell him I'll be back in a week with a court order and the constable. I'm not even sure if there is a constable, but he doesn't know either. He says something sharp in his language — I can't tell if he's saying it to me or the dogs—and disappears back into the house. I leave. I get busy at work, with the kids. So then I don't see him for weeks. Don't see the Firebird or the dogs. Which makes me feel okay. Like maybe something sank in. I drive by his house. Firebird is still in the driveway. No lights on in the house. I can hear the dogs, though. They are having at it. A real uproar.

After the UPS packages and mail piled up and the dogs kept howling, somebody calls the cops out. When they get to the front door, the smell's unmistakable. They find the guy in the den, or what's left of him, hanging from a rope, maybe a couple of feet off the floor. The dogs had likely tried to find a way out for a while. Maybe he'd even left a door open for them but the wind blew it shut (I try not to assume too much). But after four days of trying, well, there he was.

But that's not the end. Turned out he was Bosnian. He'd immigrated during the height of the war there. After a while, the cops are looking in the kitchen and they notice how uneven the floor planks are, even for an old house. They've been replaced recently. They're curious. Maybe someone had passed along a few of the neighborhood kids' stories to them. Who knows? They decide to pry up a few of the wide planks, which are old cypress. Underneath, between the joists, partially buried in the dirt, they find a girl doll the size of an infant. Its eyes and genitals have been gouged out. The cops' eyebrows rise. So they pull up other planks and find dozens more dolls laid similarly to rest, all with their eyes and genitals gouged out. So, of course, they combed the property after that, expecting to find the worst. They started digging in the backyard where a recent garden had gone in. They double-checked missing persons reports. They asked neighbors about the man. Of course now all the man's actions—his reticence, his reckless driving and weird affect, even his gypsy fortune-teller in the red velvet box—seem suspicious. Maybe harbingers of something else. But weeks go by and no bodies are found. No little girls turn up missing.

Of course, the dogs have to be destroyed.

So for a long time after, I didn't know how to feel about it. I felt partly responsible but I couldn't say exactly how. I'd scared him by posing as someone else. Was he working his way up to real girls? Or was he just a troubled man who didn't want his dogs taken away? Maybe he was fighting some terrible urge? One he'd kept in check for a long time, all the way back to Bosnia. Maybe he pretended so he didn't have to do the real thing. Maybe what he did was even heroic? We'll never know. Some stories don't have an ending even if you want them to.

26

MICHAEL DROVE UP Lake Austin Boulevard toward his dad's house. It was late. Alice was asleep in the backseat. He wasn't exactly sure why he was going. The simplest answer was that he needed money for whatever was ahead. But his brother seemed somehow mixed up in it too. With a clearer head, he might have realized it also had to do with his dad's girlfriend, Margo, whom he was a little in love with. Margo, who had bailed him out of jail several years before, who'd driven him to his probation hearing after a DUI, who'd lent him money (and inadvertently the bounty of her medicine cabinet) when his dad wouldn't speak to him. Margo, who was pregnant again after losing the first one.

He pulled into his dad and Margo's driveway and got out, careful not to wake Alice. The glow from the porch Christmas lights made everything seem temporary. He knocked several times and then Margo stood in the doorway in her robe, her belly bulging underneath. She squinted out at him, hoping to see ahead, he suspected, to whatever trouble he might have in tow. He wavered there unsteadily for a moment while she got her bearings. He'd woken her.

"Prodigal son," Margo said in a cracked voice. "You have

returned." Michael said hello, smiled in a way that felt discon-
nected from his face.

She stared at him hard. "You look like shit."

"Thanks." Her robe hung open, and he could see her belly's
navel stem poking obscenely against her nightgown, which thrilled
and embarrassed him. He tried not to look but looked anyway.
She had on a necklace, a circle of small diamonds. Her hair was
rapidly going gray.

Margo pulled her robe closed. She followed his eyes. "My
hair?" She croaked out a laugh. "Blame your sibling."

"For what?" For a few seconds Michael didn't know what they
were talking about.

"Hormones," she said, smiling. "So where's little Alice?" He
motioned with his head and she peered out at his car in the driveway. Her shoulders fell and she seemed disappointed in him.
"Bring her in. It's getting cold out."

He would make his way upstairs a little later, go through drawers, look for jewelry. He tried to remember where his dad kept
the petty cash for his movie prop runs. He ran over in his mind
the tools in the garage he might take and hock.

"You okay?" Margo said. Concern flickered through her face.

Michael thought of laying his head in Margo's lap.

"Sure," he said. He glanced at the upper floor of the house,
where he could see a light on. "My dad around?"

"You still filming out in the sticks?" Michael asked his dad. They
were sitting at the kitchen table, having some pie. The tree lights
shone from the living room, where Alice slept on the couch.
Michael realized he'd forgotten to take off the "MY NAME IS Alice"

sticker they'd given her at the police station. It had been nearly six months since Michael had seen his dad. The last time, they'd had a fight in the driveway over his keys, which his dad had taken. Darnell had pinned him against his truck after Michael punched him. The cops came out but his dad, mindful of Michael's probation, told them there had been a simple misunderstanding. The cops made notes with weary indifference. A little later, his dad, icing a welt below his eye, even made the cops coffee in the kitchen to make up for the trouble.

"On the set out in Marfa during the week and here on the weekends," his dad said. "Same old, same old." He looked at Michael's shaking hands on the kitchen table until Michael put them in his lap. Michael had helped his dad with movie props in his workshop when he was younger, his dad's hands guiding his, sliding four-by-sixes along the table saw. For one movie, they'd built a 1930s replica of an old Lucky Strike cigarettes sign that welcomed baseball fans.

"Thought you might retire, with the baby coming and all," Michael said.

"They'll have to pry the props from my cold, stiff hands," his dad said. He grinned.

Margo came into the kitchen, leaned over Darnell, and cut a slice of pie. "The new movie's a murder mystery," Margo said. "Your dad's an extra."

"No shit?" Michael said absently.

"Credited as 'Guy Peeping in Window,' " his dad said, cutting another piece of pie.

"He hardly has to act at all," Margo said.

Darnell stood up, walked behind Margo, and kissed the top of her head. "The plot is so goddamned complicated. Doubt the writers know who the murderer is. Might end up being me."

Margo's mother, Olive, eased her way through the living room toward the kitchen. She was eighty-six, nearly blind, and suffering from dementia. With the fingers of her left hand she followed the wood trim along the wall, pacing herself until she came on Alice asleep on the couch. She seemed confused. Michael wondered if Margo's mother knew where she was. Whose house? What year? Was this her daughter?

Michael got up from the table and said hello, took the old woman's hand. She looked at him and smiled. Touched his face. "Are you from the planet of men?" she asked.

"See? Mother recognizes you," Margo said.

Michael knew that Margo's mother had been in the movies, like Margo's dad. She'd been a Miss Texas runner-up in her late teens. "Quite the looker," Margo had said. "Leggy and quick-eyed." Just after World War II and before she met Margo's dad, Olive appeared in some Italian films and was even courted by a former Italian submarine commander. "Should have taken that offer," Margo had said. "Mussolini had softened him up." Later, back in America, she had small parts in B movies. Science fiction mostly. *The Unearthly,* and *Queen of Outer Space* with Zsa Zsa Gabor. They'd watched them on video. Michael remembered the space queen wearing a glittery harlequin mask because she'd been horribly disfigured by radiation burns. They recycled all the props from earlier movies like *Forbidden Planet,* his dad said, so everything supposedly otherworldly seemed tawdry and familiar.

"Sure, she recognizes him," Darnell said, nodding at Michael. "He's from the planet of men."

"Shush," Margo said.

Margo walked over and took her mother gently by the elbow, walked her to the table, eased her down in a chair. Olive's movements seem to take an eternity, as if each film cell was advancing one by one.

"How did you get past our sentries?" Olive asked Michael.

"They just opened the door," Michael said, smiling stupidly.

Olive seemed to run this over in her mind.

"Mother, would you like some pie? It's mincemeat."

"Is that child yours?" Olive asked Michael, glancing at the couch where Alice slept with her mouth open.

"Yes. That's Alice," Michael said.

"My daughter has conceived," Olive said. She had an excited, perplexed look on her face. She looked at Margo, and Margo smiled, putting a hand to her belly. Olive said, "No one knows how it happened."

"We have our suspicions," Darnell said, winking, handing Michael a cup of coffee.

Olive leaned in toward Michael. She narrowed her eyes at him. "Do you know what it is to be a woman?"

Michael shook his head.

"It means to be filled up inside yourself but to always feel empty."

"Ah," Michael said. He looked over at Margo, who was staring at Alice, worry darkening her face.

"That must be why the sentries let you pass." Olive appeared to stitch it all together in her mind. "We're a lonely planet."

Margo brought her mother a piece of pie, leaned over Michael's shoulder. She had a sweet citrus smell, maybe orange rinds.

"Of course, Queen Yllana will have to be told," Olive said, with resignation in her voice. She patted Michael's hand on the table.

"It's only right," Darnell said solemnly.

Michael sipped his coffee.

"So," Darnell said, turning to Michael, his head tilted with exaggerated curiosity. "You need some money?"

Michael carried Alice upstairs to the guest room and put her in the bed. She was breathing heavily and talking in her sleep. He wandered down the hall to his dad and Margo's room. When he flipped on the light, everything seemed brightly colored and foreign. A new painting hung over the bed. A fuzzy red cube coming out of a black void. On the dresser, opened boxes with pastel baby clothes under tissue paper. Framed photos of Darnell and Margo camping at Big Bend. Black-and-white Hollywood publicity shots of Margo's mom and dad—his dark, high cheekbones like Margo's. A photo of gap-toothed Michael as a kid in his baseball uniform. Alongside it, a photo of him and Andrew sitting together along the roofline of one of the houses his dad built back when he was a contractor. Andrew is smiling goofily at the camera but also thinking how best to show off, how to frighten everyone by pretending to fall and then twisting and swinging gracefully to the ground. Unhurt, whole. It might have been right after this photo was taken that Michael, trying to imitate him, had slipped off that same roof and broken his arm.

In a wooden jewelry box on the dresser Michael found two pairs of gold earrings and a bracelet with diamond inset. A pair of vintage gold cuff links that he suspected were Margo's dad's. He went through the other drawers quickly. Surveyed the medicine cabinet and selected a small handful of Vicodin and Xanax. Just enough to get him by for a few days. Temporary. It was all temporary.

"So, where you headed?" His dad asked after Margo had taken her mother to bed and they were alone in the kitchen.

"Nowhere."

His dad studied him. "The detectives came by," he said. "I didn't tell Margo."

"What are we talking about here?" Michael asked.

"They wouldn't say what it was about. They just said they wanted to talk to you."

"Must have missed a meeting with my probation officer."

"Son."

"I don't know. I'll call him. Sort it out."

"Son."

"What?"

"How much money do you need?"

"I'm fine."

"What about Alice?"

"She's fine too."

"We can take care of her. Until you sort out whatever it is."

Michael tapped the table leg with the side of his foot. "No, see, Lucinda's got lawyers involved now. She'd use this against me."

"Son."

"You keep saying that."

His dad rubbed his mouth, looked around the kitchen for something but seemed to forget what it was.

"Do you talk to Mom ever?" Michael asked.

"Not all that often. She's still in Chicago with the ocularist."

"Never, you mean."

"Your mom seems quite happy."

"You don't know a thing about her."

"For the longest time I thought she wouldn't move past it."

Michael resettled himself in the chair, felt the tabs of Vicodin kick in, push the worry to the distant edges of things. His dad's hand on the coffee cup seemed small and full of mischief. "I miss Andrew sometimes," Michael said. He held his hands in his lap to keep them from shaking.

"He loved you. He really did," his dad said. "Brothers don't ever say those things. But he looked out for you." His dad was looking right at him but didn't seem to see him.

Upstairs something scraped across the wood floor. Margo moving furniture around. "So, which is it, boy or girl?" Michael asked.

"Don't know. We asked the doctor not to tell us," his dad said. "It'll be a surprise."

"Thought of any names yet?" Michael asked.

"After we lost the last one we decided to wait on that."

They were quiet, listening to Margo's feet squeaking on the floor above their heads. It sounded to Michael like something straining, about to give way.

"You've got a child of your own to look after," his dad said.

Margo's citrusy smell was still in the kitchen. Michael looked out the window but all he saw were the reflected, indistinct faces of two men at a table.

27

BEFORE WE CAN make forgetful shapes with our mouths, Meredith is off, galloping toward her dad's back pasture. He's burning brush back there. Clearing land. A backhoe and several pickups full of Mexican day workers are parked nearby. Her dad speaks abruptly to them in Spanish. He's paid these men to dig a fire perimeter along both fence lines, water down the stable roof and outbuildings. Maybe they respect him, maybe they don't. There's a county burn ban because of the dry conditions, thirty-mph wind gusts, but her dad is adamant. *Today's the day.* The land already surveyed and sold to a wealthy high-tech couple who will perch their house high on the creek bluff. Her dad still has her sister to put through college, legal bills from land deals gone sour. But today is our anniversary (isn't it always?) and his mind is smoldering with Meredith. He squints into the morning cold. The sun flares off the metal roof of an outbuilding. The burning cedar sends sparks and smoke above the tree line. A hawk circles overhead. In the air around her dad, atoms vibrate. He knows these are all loose affiliations, but thinks maybe there's something to them. *Signs.* The horses, grazing in the neighbor's pasture, look back at him as if to confirm it. Most things perplex him these days. A world in which things just happen is beyond hurt somehow, beyond redemption.

Meredith's breathing is the horse's breathing, her rising and falling his. She imagines a fist-size space between her and the saddle and keeps her center of gravity just there, poised over an imaginary point, a point whose center is everywhere, bounded by nothing.

We feel slippage, our hairstyles regress, teeth grow crooked and gapped, chests flatten. *Horsey girl, come back to us,* we say.

Her dad, as always, conjures up Meredith riding alone through the blue stem grass, working her way down to the creek, where the air grows thick and damp below the limestone bluffs. Hooves clatter and slip on wet stone. There's slippage in him, too, and he hears the grinding sound that has kept him up nights and makes him worry about his sanity. It rises from everywhere at once and he thinks for some reason of the earth's tectonic plates moving against each other. He often smokes a joint and paces on the back porch in the middle of the night to rid his head of it. *They can make a real ruckus, can't they?* our horsey girl says to him. But her face is dusky, indistinct.

He realizes it's the horses. They're anxious, grinding their teeth. Maybe someone has cinched their girths too tight, he thinks. He looks over at the horses along the fence line chewing on some half-eaten apples the workers have given them. Unsaddled, unbridled. He feels a distance growing in himself, a permanent horizon that he walks toward but never reaches. A standing wave in a vast sea of tall grass. He turns around in the back pasture and for a few seconds has no idea where he is. The tree line is to the west, he tells himself. He notes this detail in blue ink on his palm.

In a copy of the handwritten autopsy report, which Meredith's dad forced himself to read, the medical examiner made note of the crescent-shaped scar on Meredith's abdomen, where she'd had surgery after the mare kicked her. One of her kidneys lost. The examiner listed the scar's measurements. The examiner described and measured, with a discreet tenderness, bruises, abrasions, bullet wounds, burns. There was a kind of reverence, her dad thought, even in the description of the ligature and bindings. Here and there, the examiner's pen had seemed to hesitate on the paper, cross through ill-considered thoughts, as if he was lost in the miniature detail of cotton fibers, fingernail clippings, and hair follicles that made up the whole.

> Ligature (underwear) shows signs of wear; partly bitten through. Matching synthetic fibers found between left bottom incisor and canine teeth. Long coarse hair found twined in wrist bindings (brassiere). Ginger colored. Likely from the tail or mane of a horse.

A tremor runs through Gumshoe's withers, and Meredith knows he is worried for her. He doesn't like the going back. "Meredith, don't let this harden your heart," her mother says to her now on the edge of her squeaky bed somewhere, and we know this was the night after Meredith had gone to the quarry and seen Melissa Sutfin blowing Marcus Bell in the back of his Jeep Cherokee. The quarry, which isn't a quarry at all but only a long gash in somebody's stony field, someone's plans gone south.

Meredith feels her own humiliation rising up through the fissures in the rock. The bed squeaks but it sounds like a leather saddle. Her mother's hand touches Meredith's cheek and her wrist smells of Dolce & Gabbana Light Blue perfume. *He's just a boy,* her mother says, though it's not her mother's face at all now but some young woman dressed as a hotel maid, with a face that's lumpy and indistinct like a feather pillow. Then her mother's face emerges beneath it. Her mother's nails are neatly manicured and painted sea green. *You're bound for better things,* she says. Her mother strokes her withers, grooms her. Meredith nuzzles her hand. Vows to forget him. To forget everything. "Oh, Meredith," her mother says, tilting her head. "Not everything. Just some things."

It strikes Meredith as strange that there could have been a time before she was, a time when she observed nothing and needed nothing, had no presence on the earth. The loud absence of herself suddenly surrounds Meredith, and it startles her.

Horsey girl, come back! we say. *We miss you so.*

She ignores us. Rides on.

Along the tree line, the cicadas start up their whine. Here and there she hears the call of a chuck-will's-widow. Meredith can smell the water in the creek. Along its eroded bank, she's found clamshell fossils, spiraled mollusk shells, a nautilus. All of this a shallow sea once, her dad had told her. So far back that it had to be imagined. Meredith's mother told her on a camping trip that she had imagined Meredith before she even became pregnant. How she made a kind of emotional space where Meredith would fit, like rolling aside in the bed for someone you know is coming. But her mother worried, too, because she and her own mother were so close that she was afraid their relationship would never measure up. *Such foolishness,* Meredith's mother would tell her. *As if you could proportion how you love.* Strangers commented on how alike they were. How even their posture was similar, their pigeon-toed walks. Meredith knows now. People she loves become strangers and strangers become achingly familiar, as if she's somehow misplaced the memories of their time together. (We don't have the heart to tell her our heads are soggy from walking on the bottom of this shallow sea.) When they'd ride down to the cabin ruins near the property line, Meredith's dad would tell her stories about settler children captured by Comanche who were adopted by the tribe and gradually forgot their life before. They lived a life of constant movement and deprivation, he said. Later, when these captives were recaptured or ransomed and returned to their relatives, they often found they had no life at all back in the civilized world. They'd forgotten the language, hated to be settled in one place. They would run away, trying to rejoin their captors, the very ones who'd massacred their families. Her dad looked bewildered then as he often did now. His how and why never adding up. *People need to belong somewhere, I guess,* he'd said, his face pinching into silence and distance. *And it's not always in the places you'd think.*

In her dad's eyes, she can see a standing wave of fire poised over the land.

28

How can you make a story from what you don't know? You just give us some ash and bits of drywall. A bridle. You say, well, there they are, see what you can do with them.

Shame on you. Shame.

Did my girls put you up to this?

29

J ACK HAD JUST gotten back from his run when he saw the
note from Sam. She was on a date and wouldn't be back until
later that night. There was a plate for him in the fridge. Sam
always felt she had to cook for him, tell him to eat. He'd lost
nearly twenty-five pounds over the last four months, almost down
to his college weight. He'd told Sam this and tugged at the waist
of his new jeans as if it was a good thing. Skin and bones, she said.
A Holocaust victim.

His wife, an optimist until the end, would have said that he
needed to right his ship, not take people down with him. She also
wouldn't have forgotten to make the house payment the last two
months, or blanked on Carla's birthday. He and Carla had split up
three months ago. She'd had enough. He was talking in his sleep
again, up at strange hours. *It's awful crowded in there,* she'd said,
motioning to his head. *No room for me.* They'd split up twice
before, but this time she'd put a down payment on a condo near
the park. In Jack's mind, he saw Sam shaking her head like Carla
did. Had it come to this? he wondered.

He'd tried to right the ship. A few weeks before she left, Carla
stood in this very kitchen while he made them breakfast, her
breasts pushing at the V of her robe. In her hair, a sequined sea

horse hair clip he'd gotten for Sam years ago in Islas Mujeres. Carla had found it among some old photos shoved in a bathroom drawer.

"Let's go to Mexico," he said. "I'm thinking a couple of nights out of this heat would do us good."

"Right." She held out her plate. "I can see you've put some real thought into it."

Spooning eggs onto her plate, he could see the slight crook to her nose where he'd hit her trying to put out the fire in his sleep.

He leaned in, kissed her on the mouth. Sam could hold down the fort, he said.

She seemed to think about this. "She's dating someone, you know."

"She doesn't tell me a thing."

"I met him. Seems nice. Thoughtful. Maybe a little old for her."

"Great. Older is good. But not too old."

"Says the man with the much-younger girlfriend."

"Twelve years apart? That's nothing," he said, setting down the pan. "In a few years it will seem more like fifteen." He smiled, cupped one of Carla's breasts with his hand, but she pulled away.

"He seems to really care for her." She looked hard at him.

"Well, that's good," he said, failure creeping in.

"I think it is," she said. She sat down at the table, started eating.

"No dreamy-eyed kid," he said.

"No, not this one. And he's polite. You know, in that fake southern way you like. Chivalrous."

"Perhaps I shall have to make this gentleman's acquaintance,"

Jack said, raising his eyebrows. "To determine if his intentions are honorable." He paced out a few steps in the kitchen, turned, aimed the spatula at an imaginary opponent across the room.

Carla grinned. "Jack Dewey's finally here to defend our honor, ladies. Cue the collective swoon."

30

I think people are looking in the wrong places. That's my feeling. Lots of pressure on the police, understand. Three young white girls. They're going to find someone. They're going to find someone because that's the story they're telling. The story they're telling those girls' parents. The public. The one they're telling themselves. They march some unlucky motherfucker in braces out in front of the cameras, say take a look at that. We in control now. But somebody's out there telling a bigger story. And this bigger story makes the other one look small. In fact, the smaller story's already a part of the bigger story and doesn't know it. Can't see it. Can't pick it out of a lineup. Why? Because evil don't look like anything.

You know why we got all those moon towers? Like the one at Zilker Park they string all the lights on to make into a Christmas tree? They put those up in the 1890s after seven women—five of them black—were raped and murdered. Mutilated. One beheaded. One with an ice pick jammed through the ear. Servant girl annihilator, that writer O. Henry called it. That was before they hauled his ass away to jail for supposedly embezzling money from a bank. Stupid motherfucker got on the wrong side of somebody. I'll say this: He got murdered black girls in the newspaper. How often does that happen? So, after the murders, the city starts a curfew. A few people arrested, prosecuted, the husband of one of the murdered white women gets acquitted at trial. They don't have any evidence, no real motive, but they try to tell a story anyway. Folks are still scared. They keep their kids out of the front yard. Don't go out at night. So they try another story: Why don't we make night into day? Put up a fake moon?

31

THIS IS WHAT Truck and Trailer told Hollis:
Down where the springs gush from the dam, they'd met a young man who asked about Hollis. The young man was walking along a creek path choked with honeysuckle and clouds of bees. He was smooth-shaven (shiny, Trailer had said, like a baby) and dressed in a white dress shirt and tie like a missionary, a leather satchel draped over a shoulder. A motley-colored dog trotted behind him, but they couldn't say if it was his. The young man paused next to their camp and gave them some breakfast tacos in a paper bag. He sat on a rock and watched them eat, seeming to take pleasure in their appetites. When Trailer winced from his bad tooth, the young man suggested a tincture of clove oil until he could see a dentist. He asked them about the area but seemed to know the neighborhoods already. He spoke about the natural beauty of the landscape. Live oaks and cypress. Told them the hills all around were once a mountain range that was beaten down by a sea. Those mountains, he said, were still down there, moving, sending tremors in the earth.

Hearing this, Truck and Trailer nodded and chewed. The young man was a gentleman and a scholar, Truck said. Trailer said that the young man had a peculiar way of talking. Like someone standing a ways off but whispering in your ear.

"You some kind of missionary?" Trailer had asked the man.

"No, nothing like that," the young man said, and smiled as if he was pleased they thought so.

"Aren't you hot in that getup?" Truck asked him, motioning to his tie.

The young man, staring off through a break in the trees at the creek, didn't seem to hear. "Do you gentlemen know a Mr. Finger?" he asked, but in a casual way, as if he could take or leave the answer.

Truck and Trailer nodded but stopped chewing.

"Hollis, you mean?" Trailer said.

"Yes," he said. "Hollis."

"Hollis hurt his head in Iraq," Truck said, excusing Hollis his many trespasses.

"That's why I need to talk to him."

"To help him?" Trailer asked.

"That's right," the man said. "I'd like to offer a little help here and there." The young man's forehead gleamed. His cheeks were flushed. He picked up a small, flat piece of limestone and tossed it toward the creek, where it struck the surface several times and disappeared.

"You with the VA?" Truck asked, squinting up at his bright face.

Wind blew high in the trees, but the air close to the ground was stifling. Truck said for some reason he thought the motley dog, which lay motionless on its side on a slab of rock, had died.

And then a tremor went through its body that made him think it might be whelping puppies.

"You with us or against us?" Trailer said, wiping a clump of egg from his mouth.

"That's enough, Arthur," Truck said quietly.

"It's okay," said the man. "You're just looking out for your friend."

"Hollis ain't done nothing to nobody," Trailer said.

The man said he was sure that was true, that sometimes things got confused and had to be turned inside out to be understood. And even then they wouldn't always give up their mystery. He said he knew a man who once set fire to a whole apartment building out of love. The man had immolated himself in his lover's bed.

"I don't get you," Truck said.

The young man threw another stone and it skipped silently across the creek.

"Immolated?" Trailer asked. "Set himself on fire?"

"That's right," the young man said. "He couldn't be separated from her. A moth to the flame, so to speak."

"People died in this fire? Besides him?"

The young man seemed to think about this for a second. "It was a very fierce love," he said.

The dog now started barking at something scuttling in the underbrush, an armadillo or possum, and the young man tossed it something from his pocket to quiet it. He pulled a flask from his satchel, took a drink, and passed it to Truck and Trailer. They sipped on the whiskey for a bit. The young man seemed cheerful but mindful of their qualms, Truck told Hollis. At this stage of the telling it became unclear to Hollis whether or not they'd told the young man about Hollis's sleeping in his art car on side streets, or his trips below the gushing spring to swim and bathe, or his recent visions of the girls, though Hollis had pressed them on these points.

After they'd drunk most of the whiskey, Truck and Trailer said the young man told them a story about Judas from a gospel they'd never heard of. In this gospel, Judas didn't betray Jesus at all. In this story, Judas is the only disciple who understands Jesus's true teachings and his own role in turning things inside out. In this story, Judas is the hero because he brings about Jesus's suffering, frees him from the terrible clothing of his body. The young man said that this was the fiercest love of all.

Truck told Hollis he felt the hair on the back of his neck rise. He said he didn't say anything for a minute or so because his head was buzzing with the whiskey, his heart thudding too fast. He could hear the creek rushing clear and cool over the rocks below them. Then he saw that the young man had an erection.

Trailer told Hollis he knew all along that the man was a missionary.

32

THE VIDEO OF the ice cream shop is a glimpse into another world. A canvas painted by a master, rolled up and spirited away, then rediscovered by chance in somebody's attic. The woman, Theresa Mooney, lives in Houston. She'd forgotten where the video was taken, she told Rosa Heller on the phone. She'd visited her sister in Austin that December to help her move after the sister and her husband had separated. So she'd held an impromptu sixth birthday for her son with his cousins in an ice cream shop not far from where her sister lived. She'd forgotten the name. Her sister's trouble back then had colored everything. She wouldn't have remembered anything if it wasn't for the photo of one of the girls in the article Rosa had written on the fifth anniversary of the murders. Elizabeth, her name tag says in the video. Elizabeth had helped with the birthday party, made balloon animals, even shot some video of the birthday boy and his cousins. She appears at the 1 minute 51 second mark on the DVD, which Theresa Mooney recently found in some boxes, its case mislabeled as X-MAS PARTY. In the video, the focus is off. Theresa Mooney is still learning to use the camera. Zoom or not zoom. Elizabeth is hamming it up a bit, making balloon crowns and swords. Zoom and you see small scars on her hands as they twist and twist, this way, the other. A Lyle Lovett song is playing in the background somewhere.

Theresa Mooney's son Dean's striped shirt already has a smudge of chocolate ice cream down the front. He sticks out his tongue. Theresa tells Rosa about the little scar under his chin where he fell four feet off the porch when he was two because she was distracted. *Down he went,* she says, a moment still frozen in her mind.

On the tape, in a wider shot, you can see that it's dark out, likely still early evening by the crowd. The windows and double doors at the front of the shop reflect back the interior. If you enlarge the DVD image, as Rosa has, you can see several things: at the counter, the other two girls are working. Meredith's head is down, counting out change but thinking about boys, Rosa imagines. Or maybe her horse. A misplaced bridle or brush. Zadie with her ponytail at the drive-through window. The oldest and dreamiest of the girls. If you enlarge the image more, you can see Zadie moving her hips, swaying to a tinny song that's playing on a car stereo in the drive-through line. It's hard to tell what song it is at first, but if you replay it several times, like Rosa, you can tell it's a cover of "Sea of Love." *Do you remember when we met?*, a line that plays in Rosa's head for weeks after. The reflection of Zadie leans out in the drive-through window, laughs with her hand to her mouth as if she's been caught being herself.

Here, you might suddenly remember, as Rosa did, that these reflections aren't like photo negatives, not images of us flipped left to right; they're images of us reversed front to back, as if looking at a mask turned inside out.

You can see other things in the window's reflection at the 2:46

mark: near the front counter, behind the table where a woman and a bearded man are spooning ice cream to their mouths, are two men, one in a long overcoat. The man in the overcoat is sipping from his shake. There's glare on the window where their faces should be.

In the foreground of the video, at the 3:11 mark, one of the big balloons slips out of Elizabeth's hands, makes a farting sound, then curlicues in the air. The birthday partiers giggle. When she goes to retrieve it, the camera follows her and the two men rise from the table but turn away. One of them, the one in the overcoat, his back to the camera, presents the deflated balloon to Elizabeth with a chivalrous bow, as if returning a lost glove.

33

W E'RE SEVEN EIGHT nine ten eleven twelve and our
mother is driving us to Galveston. Every August we'd
stay in a beach house on stilts that our Nana owned. Galveston is
no fancy-pants like Corpus Christi, our Nana would say. It's real.
Things get washed away here. When we see the city limits signs,
we sing the Glen Campbell song until we're hoarse. Around the
tenth time our mother says if we don't stop she'll turn around,
head back to Austin, where it's sweltering and there is no beach.
She means it, she says. She's got a splitting headache because she
and Ray have been fighting. Another of us, the horsey girl, is in
the front passenger seat, but our mother just ignores her like she
does. She's made her a white space on the wall because it's just
too much, she says. But we say it isn't enough. *We're together,* we
say. She pokes at us in the backseat with an old umbrella and
we say, *Oh, wow, thanks, Mom, you punctured a tendon in our arm or
something.* But then we quiet down and hum the rest of the Glen
Campbell song to ourselves and watch her eyes in the rearview.
Weather her mood. It rains as it always does here in the afternoon,
and the water branches out in little rivulets on the backseat car
windows, like arteries or roots feeding something or nothing.
Behind these, turquoise, violet, orange wooden beach houses

flicker by, and we think how beautiful it all is. That even if it was all made up, we'd want it anyway. Like looking forward to watching a terrific movie again even as you're watching it. *The Birds* is our favorite. *Have you ever seen so many gulls? What do you suppose it is?* We scream every time just before the dumbass blows himself up at the gas station. Laugh until ginger ale comes out our nose. Watching our mother's eyes in the rearview, we can tell she is thinking of the Halloween we dressed her up as the actress Tippi Hedren, papier-mâché crows with wire feet perched high in the blond wig we got from the school's theater prop room. *Shut the door,* we hear our mother say in her spunky Tippi Hedren voice. *They'll get in. Shut the door!*

34

You're leaving out so much.

What about the part when we went to Galveston when the girls were small and my mother answered the door and she pretended not to know them? I don't know any Zadie or Elizabeth, she said. Their names don't ring a bell. Maybe you can describe them for me? And the girls turning to each other, round-eyed in amazement.

IV

35

THE WEEK AFTER the Christmas party, Kate had driven by Jack Dewey's house dozens of times. Parked outside, some nights. Watched him disappear and reappear in windows that he seemingly never bothered to cover. Once she fell asleep in the driver's seat and was startled awake when the paperboy missed his aim and struck her car with a thwack. She'd been dreaming of the girls again. They were being disagreeable. She'd said some terrible things to them, had woken up ashamed. In the dream, she was letting out their prom dresses, using a seam ripper with its tiny sharp hook along the stitching. The girls stood on chairs in the kitchen, which was also Kate's mother's kitchen in Galveston, except for some reason the floor had a funny slope to it so all the fruit rolled up the counter. Kate's mother sat at the kitchen table in a blue flowered dress, playing Scrabble, ignoring them. Every time Kate tried to get her girls to stay put for a new measurement, they'd shift their feet or add a few pounds or begin to crumble and smoke there on the chairs with their arms out to their sides. Kate's hand shook. How thoughtless. *Didn't they know she had better goddamn things to do with her evenings?* She threw the seam ripper and it stuck in the wall by the calendar, a tiny harpoon. Her girls looked at each other with round eyes, stifling a laugh.

Jack was on a three-on, four-off schedule at his station. On his off days, he would run in the evenings, circling the park. After, he'd bike to Deep Eddy Bar or the Horseshoe Lounge. He was working on a project of some sort, judging by the building materials in the garage, the tarp-covered stack of wood on the side of the house. He ate at odd hours, she thought, drank too much. When his daughter wasn't there, he'd often turn all the lights on in the middle of the night, as if the house was bustling with activity. She heard him playing the piano sometimes at night, though slowly, ploddingly, as if he'd just picked it up and didn't have much of an ear. A few times she'd braved the backyard and crouched in the honeysuckle that had taken over his fence line. The new perspective, its distances and proportions, excited her blood and made her dizzy. She could see the blur of his head in the frosted bathroom window, when he was showering. Once, she saw him masturbating in a nice mid-century chair in his bedroom. She didn't turn away.

Now, in the long living room window, she can see paint cans, drop cloths, a toolbox. He'd apparently taken off the old paneling recently and replaced it with maple bead board. Painted the walls sea green, sanded and stained the wood floors a dark pecan. Framed photos hung in the hallway. She could see a senior-year photo of Jack's daughter, Samantha.

Later, she'll think how her body knew before her head did. Crouched low in the honeysuckle, her legs began to tremble. It took her several seconds to realize she was looking at a replica of her old living room.

36

J ACK FEELS ALONG the nylon search rope in his head, fingers
the knots he's remembered to tie at intervals, finds the girls.

You should call Kate, Elizabeth says.

I'm afraid.

She's not getting any younger, Zadie says.

I keep thinking things will get better, that I'll snap out of it.

All that smoke and water makes your head soggy, Elizabeth says.

When I was in sixth grade, Jack says, *we moved to Temple, Texas. I
was just miserable. Didn't know anybody. I used to run away from school
every few weeks, head out into a cotton field past the field house. Hide
there in the irrigation ditches until school was out, making up another life
in my head.*

We know just the place, Meredith says.

Tell us a story, Zadie says, in Jack's daughter's voice.

I liked the ones about the Texas explorers, Jack says. *Coronado in the
panhandle. Cabeza de Vaca living with the cannibals.*

Everyone naked and mosquito-bit, Elizabeth says. She shudders.

What kind of parent names their child Cow Head? Meredith says.

Tell us a story, Zadie says. *One we'll remember.*

Cabeza de Vaca is shipwrecked on Galveston Island, Jack says.
Almost all his men lost. The Karankawa find him and three others there

on the beach. They weep at the men's suffering. Then the Karankawa enslave them for two years.

Sounds like theater work, Zadie says.

Cheery story, Meredith says. *When do they get eaten?*

Galveston, oh Galveston, Elizabeth sings.

Cabeza de Vaca and his men stoke the smudge fires for the Karankawa to keep mosquitoes away. Soot in their nostrils and eyes all night long. Their skin dried, blackened.

Barbecue de Vaca, Zadie says.

Then one day, a day that will change everything, Cabeza de Vaca, he saves one of the Karankawa. Makes an incision in the injured man's chest with a knife and removes an arrowhead pressing against his heart. The Karankawas' eyes widen in amazement and fear. But before Cabeza de Vaca stitches him back up, he's shocked to see other things in the man's chest cavity. An opal class ring Cabeza de Vaca's wife, Maria, had lost years before. A flesh-colored hearing aid. A stick of her pink coral lipstick. Her ivory-handled seam ripper. Cabeza de Vaca, always the showman, holds the objects from another world in his hand for everybody to see.

Zadie and Elizabeth cover their mouths in mock surprise.

Meredith rubs the scar along her abdomen.

After he's stitched up, the Karankawa man opens his eyes. Rises. His dark skin shimmers with grease and soot. The air around him vibrates with a future he almost didn't have.

The sun hammers Cabeza de Vaca's bare chest until it shines like armor.

Meredith fans her face. *Quite the hottie,* she says.

One of our mothers isn't sleeping much these days, they all say. *She's waiting.*

The Karankawa, Jack says, *gather around Cabeza de Vaca, their faces tight, and demand to know whether this is a good thing or a bad thing.*

Tough crowd, Elizabeth says

You know how to whistle, don't you? Zadie says to Jack in her best Lauren Bacall. *You just put your lips together and blow.*

37

THE HIDEOUS MAN set fire to Hollis's car. He couldn't say exactly when this was. All his lovely things, gone. Books and maps and photos of the girls. All his talismans. In the backseat, Hollis had propped up his sleeping bag and pillow and blanket like the figure of a sleeping man. He'd hidden in the woods and waited. The fire, fueled by his possessions, was very bright.

38

O N THE PHONE, the caller said he'd read Rosa's column. He said he thought he might be able to help. Might be able to identify the men on the DVD she'd found. He'd been in the shop that day. Could he see the video? The caller wouldn't leave his name. He seemed young and distracted. At points during the conversation his voice seemed to fall off a cliff. *Hello?* she'd say. And then he'd fetch it back.

He told her a rambling story about an airplane crash. A baby cried in a field. Someone was lost. Someone came back. It made no sense.

Sir, she interrupted, *can I ask you something? Why now? If you were in the shop, why wait until now to come forward? Have you called the tip line?*

The caller said he was a father now and often thought about the girls. Then he said something that tumbled into the void, a tiny thing way down there.

Sir? she said. She could hear a child's singsong voice in the background.

You have to tell the story, he said finally.

Blood thudded in Rosa's ears.

39

THREE YEARS AFTER Michael's parents divorced, when he was seventeen, his mother, Kay, met a man, an ocularist— a maker of prosthetic eyes—remarried, and moved to Chicago. She and Michael didn't talk much anymore. A phone call at the holidays, Alice's birthday, his own. Festive occasions, his mother called them. When she visited them in Austin once, they'd gone to the Zilker Botanical Gardens and Alice fed the koi in the pond. Michael's mother wanted Alice to hug her and call her Grammy, but the heat had made Alice red-faced and irritable. She wanted Alice to try on clothes at the mall, but it was near Alice's nap time and so they'd said their good-byes at the Ruby Tuesday while Alice wailed inconsolably about a stuffed tiger kitten that he'd later find wedged in the backseat of the car. Pulling away from them in the parking lot, his mother's eyes shone with need, and it pained him to remember the way he and Andrew had always taken advantage of her, telling even transparent lies because she would believe anything.

Kay lived in a Chicago neighborhood called Ravenswood. She and the ocularist had gotten a great deal on a house not far from Lake Michigan, she'd told him a month ago. He should bring Alice for a visit in the summer, she said. Alice would love the beach, the aquarium, the Lincoln Park Zoo. His mother even mentioned Lucinda, saying she'd recently been in touch, asking Kay to send her some photos of Alice. We talked just like two mothers, she'd said, her voice brightening.

When Michael and Alice drove into Chicago it was late morning and he could feel the cold through the windows. Snow swirled in the road ahead of them. In the distance, low clouds halved the skyscrapers downtown. He'd never been to Chicago, and as they drove in on Interstate Fifty-Five and turned onto Lake Shore Drive, the sheer size of the city struck him. It seemed to go on and on, bounded by nothing except Lake Michigan, which was more like an inland sea.

He'd spoken with his mother before they left his dad's, and she'd seemed irritated with him, but she'd covered quickly with talk of Alice. There was always a place there for them, she said. Still, she needed to talk to her husband, the ocularist, since his daughter, Elise, was graduating from DePaul that weekend. A little hectic, she said, but doable. She would make it work. It was a treat, an early Christmas present, she said, worry pinching her voice. Alice, picking up on the conversation, loudly dictated her Christmas list. Michael felt the room tilt a little, panic flutter through him. His dad had even spoken to his mother for a few minutes, his voice softening as if speaking to a child. He'd turned away from Michael while talking to her, but now and then he'd look over, widen his eyes in mock frustration. On the drive to Chicago, Michael had called his mother twice and left messages, saying they'd be there a day sooner than planned, but he hadn't heard back.

Why had he called the reporter the day before they left? Out of guilt? Fear? He couldn't be sure. He was worried about the video. Was he sitting at one of the tables? Standing in line? It was somehow tangled up with his dead brother, disquieting dreams about a baby crying in a field. A part of him wanted to confess to the reporter things he'd never done.

In the backseat, Alice was playing a game with her dolls and looking up every few minutes, saying, It's snowing and there's a bridge and there's a man walking across it and there's a ship way down in the water but it has sunk right there and is not moving no matter what people say and the man is wearing a red scarf and it's cold out and I'm hungry for a Nutella sandwich and a little carton of milk.

Alice was excited by the waves crashing against the storm wall along Lake Shore Drive, so they'd exited at Montrose Avenue and followed the signs to the beach parking lot, where they could get a better view. Bundled in their inadequate coats and gloves, they walked along the lake wall for a little while in the snow, Alice throwing chunks of ice into the spray and wind. "It's wonderful weather out," she said under her scarf. She made a snowball, hit him in the shoulder, and laughed. He tossed one back too high that clipped the top of her head. She put a hand to her head and started to cry and he felt his legs go weak. "Fooled you!" she said, leaping away from him and laughing.

In the distance, the lake merged with the gray horizon until he couldn't tell which was which. They were about to turn back for the car when he saw a white Mercury pull into the near-empty parking lot and make several slow loops around, as if looking for a space. Two cross-country skiers were gliding across the park. As they came alongside the parking lot, the Mercury's driver's window came down and he could see a man speaking with the skiers, his breath streaming. Then the skiers pointed to the park and then beyond it to the wall where he and Alice stood, and the skiers glided off, a little faster than they'd come, it seemed to Michael. The air was sharp in his nostrils. He took Alice's hand and they went the other way along the wall, away from the lot, careful to avoid slick spots. Far out in the lake he thought he saw the outline of a ship. After a while they circled back to the car, got in, and sat warming themselves. "My face fell asleep," Alice said, pinching her cheek. She laughed in amazement.

Michael smoked a cigarette with the window cracked. There was no sign of the white Mercury. His car was nearly out of gas. He grabbed Alice's backpack from the passenger seat—where he'd put the cash and jewelry he'd taken from his dad's house— and pulled two twenty-dollar bills from a zippered pocket. He drove slowly around the marina, its bare white piers sticking up from the water, where he imagined yachts would be moored in the summer. On them, carefree people drinking, laughing.

"I can hear your teeth back there," Andrew said. This was when Michael was twelve. They were crawling through the storm sewer, and Michael's teeth were chattering. He was cold and scared. "Would you die for me?" his brother asked him once. "I mean, if you were up on the University Tower and this crazy guy with a gun said your brother could live if you'd jump, would you do it?" Andrew was passing his thumb through a lighter flame. Michael shrugged, said he didn't know. Andrew laughed. "It's a long way down, bro."

Andrew's friend Jeff, who always messed everything up, was down in the tunnel with them. "Why is your brother such a pussy?" Jeff's voice said somewhere up ahead. Jeff was always talking about how he'd like to give it to Lisa Soto or Meghan Schmidt. Jeff had shown them some foreign porn movies once, videos that Jeff had stolen from his dad's German friend and kept in a tackle box on his closet shelf. The people in them did things to each other that seemed somehow beyond their control, as if they'd better do it or else. As if they had a gun to their heads. Everything outside wanted in and everything inside wanted out. Seen up close, the jumbled body parts looked like voracious animals or insects engaged in some fierce combat. Michael clenched his teeth, moved faster in the tunnel. Water trickled between his knees. Every few feet something brushed his face or clung to his hair and he slapped wildly at his head. He was weak and everybody could see it, Michael thought. His insides were turned out like pockets.

At one point the storm sewer tunnel widened out and the ceiling rose and became a kind of room where all the tunnels converged. It smelled bad here. A mixture of shit and turpentine. Ahead of him, Andrew's flashlight beam jittered along the floor. In one corner was a dirty twin mattress set high on plastic crates. All around, stacks of old magazines, used spray paint cans, glass jars. A camping lantern hung from a rope. Then Andrew turned his flashlight toward the ceiling, and bright shapes emerged out of the darkness. The painted naked body of a woman stretched above them. Her fleshy hips curved along a bulge in the ceiling. Oaks and cypresses grew from the dark tangle of her vagina.

Between her breasts ran the blue veins of creeks and rivers that emptied at her navel into an iridescent sea. Her lower lip was pierced with a fishhook threaded with a silver chain. Her blue eyes were cast upward, like a saint's. Michael's knees grew weak, and something inside him fell silent. For a few seconds he thought his heart had stopped beating.

"I'd fuck her," Jeff said. He laughed.

Andrew held the flashlight steady on the painted woman. The fishhook and silver chain gleamed.

Up ahead in one of the tunnels, there was a loud scuffling sound and Michael imagined a trapped animal. Its eyes burning with fear and need.

Michael remembered a family photo taken when he was six or seven. His mother is young, her hair braided in pigtails, standing with the three of them at a roadside overlook in Big Bend National Park. It's late spring. Desert flowers are in bloom. Andrew and his dad are on the right, goofing around, making wild eyes and pointing at something below. Michael is standing in front of his mother. Her tanned arms drape his chest, holding him close, as if afraid he might lose his footing.

40

THE HIDEOUS MAN. Can you tell me what he looks like?" the giantess asked Hollis. She tried to hide her stature by leaning toward him, elbows on the picnic table, but he knew. Her left eye drooped a little, almost imperceptibly. Her ear lobes were large but not gangly. Proportional. Fitting for a giantess, he thought.

"It's hard to say," Hollis said. He fingered the names of Lil' Steve and Ernesto carved into the picnic table beside her little red recorder. She said she was a reporter, not a cop, and he believed her. She laughed high in her nose (also relatively proportional) and didn't smell like fear dressed up as order. Her smell was smooth and papery.

"Other people described a young man in a long coat."

"Yes." On the table, her shadow bent toward his.

"That's who you saw?"

"There's a great commotion in his face," Hollis said.

"Commotion?"

"Like before a tremor," Hollis said. He grinned though he knew he shouldn't.

"A seizure, you mean?"

Hollis laughed. "No. Like in the earth," he said. "A tremor in the earth."

Grackles squawked from the trees.

When she smiled Hollis felt his sinuses open.

"He's hard to picture? Is that what you're saying?"

"Like before a tremor," Hollis said. "All the animals in commotion."

"Right," she said, in a voice that nudged him along. She looked at him with her giantess eyes. It was like a child's game, Hollis thought. She was waiting for him on the other side. *Red rover, red rover, won't you come over?*

"Those girls," the giantess said. "Their families. You can help them."

An invitation to a party, he thought. A gathering of friends.

The creek was rushing down below, smooth, smooth. They were swimming in it even now. It filled the shallow sea.

The sun slanted through the trees.

"He works downtown," Hollis said, though he wasn't sure how he knew this. "One of the big hotels." With his finger Hollis flicked a J-shaped piece of dried bird shit off the table. He looked at the giantess. Her eyes grew bright.

Red rover, red rover.

41

W HEN ROSA TURNED eight, her dad began dating
the woman who would later be her stepmom. A relatively happy period, she remembered. Her dad's girlfriend was in
nursing school in St. Louis, so they'd take the train from Chicago
some weekends and stay there. When they came back to their
house in Chicago one Sunday night, something was wrong. They
stood on the front porch with their suitcases and her dad put the
key in the lock and tried to open the door. But it wouldn't open.
In a strange voice, one that made her think again of the woman
lying in the field, he asked her to sit down on the steps. He pried
open the door enough to find that their bicycles and their fridge
were wedged into the narrow entryway to block the door. When
they finally got inside, they discovered that someone had broken
into the house by smashing through a floor-to-ceiling window in
the downstairs family room. It had rained while they were gone,
and water pooled on the wood floor beneath the window. The air
had a musty smell. The downstairs rooms themselves were
empty, everything stolen. The house echoed. She ran up the
stairs, where her bedroom was. Near the top landing, her father's
dark blue sport coat lay crumpled against the railing, his empty
cuff link box beside it. Her room, though, was as she'd left it. Her

treasures—her red guitar, owl bank, art easel, rock polisher and cigar boxes full of polished rocks and bottle caps—all in place. Why had they taken everything else and spared her room? Her treasures? She remembered her dad putting her to bed that night, saying that she shouldn't be scared, because the reason the thieves broke into the house was precisely because they weren't there. This made sense to her but also seemed somehow inadequate. Her dad tried to put her at ease. He'd patted her back to put her to sleep after reading to her. But she wasn't scared at all. She was amazed. All her treasures spared. It seemed a miracle. God intervening even though they weren't believers. In her mind, she saw again the scene from *The Ten Commandments* she'd watched on TV the week before, the Israelites painting lamb's blood on their doors so the shadow of death would pass them by.

Rosa's dad had been diagnosed with prostate cancer, and she flew up to Chicago to see him. The cancer wasn't advanced, but his PSA count was way up. On the phone he was lighthearted, said there wasn't anything to worry about. If you live long enough, you get it. He told her a joke: "A man goes to see his doctor for his test results and the doc says, 'I've got some bad news. You've got cancer and dementia.' The man says, 'Whew, I really dodged a bullet. I sure thought I had cancer.'" Her dad laughed. On the phone, she could hear him take a drag off a cigarette, exhale. He'd quit five years before, with the help of some drug that made you lose your sense of taste, appetite. His good spirits somehow made her feel orphaned already.

He mentioned on the phone that they were going to do some kind of targeted radiation. He wanted her there, she suspected, though he wouldn't say it. She'd intended to fly to Chicago three weeks ago, but had gotten sidetracked by her fifth anniversary story on the murders. Interviews. The video. Detective Robeson. Hollis Finger. A recent lead on the young man in the overcoat. The caller. And then right before she left, there had been a break in the case, a person of interest identified. She'd heard it from her sources in the department.

At Midway Airport, standing near the luggage carousel, her father seemed more gaunt and stooped than she remembered. He was giddy while they waited for her luggage, touching her back and shoulders from time to time as if making sure she was really there.

"You get lovelier with age."

"In the genes," she said, and smiled.

"Got that right," he said. "There's some who hold my good looks against me."

"It's lonely at the top," she said.

"I saw your mother recently. At a *Tribune* retirement party."

"Did she bring her beau? What's his name? Phillip?"

"Oh, yes, he was there. *Phillip.* Did you see that photo on his book jacket? He looks like a serial killer."

"She seems happy out in Phoenix. He treats her well."

Her dad was silent for a second. "Your car runs out of gas out in the desert and he's the one who pulls to the shoulder for you in the unmarked van. And believe me, all his teeth are perfect."

42

WHEN HE HEARD the shots from inside the ice cream shop, Michael's first thought was to run away. He'd stay at a friend's apartment for a few days, then make his way to San Antonio or Houston by bus. He thought of waving down one of the passing cars along Barton Springs Road, telling the drivers that something had gone wrong inside. Something terrible. As he walked around the side of the building toward the road, he saw, behind the drive-through window blinds, a bright, flickering light. The smell of smoke was already in the air.

He didn't do either of the things he'd thought of. The younger and older man came out the back delivery door before he could, he told himself. They were moving quickly but assuredly to the car and motioned him on. In one hand, the older man was carrying a black bag that said CHAMPION SPORTS and in the other, a light tripod. He was breathing heavily. The younger man had his long coat draped over his shoulder like someone from a magazine ad or TV commercial. He could be anyone or no one at all.

Michael had trouble looking at their faces, knowing that they could read his thoughts. They had an agreement that was inviolable. *What good are men without their word?*

He fingered the conch in his jacket pocket.

Before he got in the driver's seat, he asked the younger man what happened, why it had taken so long. He said he was worried they'd forgotten about him. The younger man gave him a disappointed look. "I would never forget you," he said. "I've carved you on the palm of my hand." Then the younger man plucked a leaf off Michael's jacket, brushed something off his shoulder. And that was when Michael saw, on the younger man's cuff, spatters of blood.

Michael got a call on his cell phone from a number he didn't recognize. He thought of the reporter, the terrifying curiosity in her voice when he'd called her.

"Michael? This is Elise." At first he drew a blank and then the name arranged itself into an image of a tall girl with dark eyes. A graduation gown, hat.

"Your mom asked me to call," she said.

"Oh, that's great," he said.

"She's with my dad at the hospital. He's got a—whadayacallit—heart arrhythmia. They're running some tests."

"Who is it, Daddy?" Alice said sleepily from the backseat. "Is it Momma?"

"Is he okay?" Michael asked.

"They think so. They think he's going to be okay." Her voice wavered a bit. "I'm sorry to hit you with this."

He felt the heaviness from the long drive, wondered why they were even here.

"Why don't I meet you somewhere?" she said, her voice righting itself. "We can get you two out of that car, find you something to eat."

"Sure, we're about past ready for that," he said, again seeing her dark hair, eyes. She mentioned a pizza place near the hospital, off Broadway Avenue.

He wondered how he might help Elise, his mother. They were in a fix. Chance had intervened and he was being asked to set things right. He looked in the backseat and Alice had fallen asleep. Her eyelids twitched, dreaming.

He and Alice parked near the L station at Wilson and Broadway, not far from the hospital. Michael wanted to get his prescription filled before meeting Elise. He'd already gone through the few tabs he'd taken from his dad. It was lunchtime, and bundled-up people hustled back and forth, off buses and into the station. The L rattled overhead, and a dusting of snow fell on them. On Broadway, he saw a tall sign that read WIGS AND HAIR. They found the pharmacy a half block away. He told Alice she could pick out a toy, something small, while he did business with the pharmacist, who looked over her glasses at him with distrust after he handed her his forged prescription. "Texas, eh?" she said. He needed a cigarette. The front door bell chimed. Otis Redding sang over the intercom. Michael smiled stupidly, told her they were here for a visit with Grandma. "Long way from home," the pharmacist said doubtfully, but smiled anyway. She looked off down an aisle where Alice was playing with some stuffed animals and a plastic dinosaur. Behind Alice, a large black woman in silver snow boots was talking with a stock boy. The pharmacist said she'd have to call the doctor for approval. Common practice for out-of-state script. It might take a little while, she said. The person who'd sold him the prescription—a bicycle mechanic with a radio voice—was supposed to answer on the other end of the phone, rattle off a combination of numbers that would lower the volume in his head.

Afterward, they walked a half block away to the pizzeria, where they'd meet Elise. It was snowing more heavily now. He held Alice's hand. The pizzeria was also a convenience store, which seemed right somehow. A Middle Eastern man with an impassive face sat behind a counter window. Small liquor bottles lined the shelf behind him. The room smelled of baked pizza crust. Chairs, tables, and a video arcade room were wedged into the back. Alice wanted to play the games, so he got quarters for her and struck up a conversation with the Middle Eastern man. Because of his accent, Michael didn't catch much of what he said, only that his children were attending Loyola.

The front door chimed. A young woman in a parka came in, and he went up to her, thinking she might be Elise, but she didn't speak English. She looked away. She paid for her pizza and left.

He felt the Vicodin begin to work away at the edges of things.

The arcade games made pinging and squawking noises.

He asked the Middle Eastern man if he'd seen a dark-haired woman, early twenties. Tall.

"Your girlfriend?" the man asked without a smile.

"No," Michael said. "My sister, actually." He looked off at Alice, feeling suddenly close to Elise but knowing it was the pills. "My stepsister," he said, correcting himself. The baked warmth of the room pressed in. Alice made a disappointed sound in the little arcade room.

"You have other siblings?"

"Yes. A brother," Michael said. "But he died."

"Unfortunate," the man said, and nodded. He seemed about to say something else, but the phone rang in the little pizzeria window at the back of the room and the man held up a finger and went over to answer it.

"Michael?" a woman's voice said, and he turned.

Elise was shorter than he thought she'd be—different from what he remembered of his mother's descriptions. Her eyebrows dark, thick. Blue eyes. Her short hair and wool hat made her look boyish. Pretty in a way that made him uneasy.

They ordered a pizza and sat at a table in the back. Alice joined them and said she was out of quarters. She sat beside Elise and drew on some stationery that Elise pulled from her purse. "How do you spell 'My Little Pony'?" Alice asked Elise, and Elise wrote it out for her in purple-crayoned letters. Other customers gathered at tables. The room grew pleasantly warm.

Elise filled him in while they ate pizza. Mentioned her father's shortness of breath at her graduation the night before, his mother's concerns. His mother's hands shaking so badly that the cabbie thought she was the one who was ill. Elise had joined them both at the hospital. There was a vagueness to all of it, Michael thought, that only left-out people could feel.

Elise said that there would be more tests today. Michael and Alice could come up to visit the hospital room this afternoon and cheer them up, she said. She looked off at people passing on the sidewalk in the snow, then back at Michael. She squeezed his hand on the table. "I'm glad you're here," she said, and smiled. Alice looked up from her drawing and said, "What about me?"

When Elise and Alice went off to play video games, Michael

headed for the bathroom. Standing at the urinal, he could hear thumping and groaning in the pipes. His piss had a sharp chemical smell. The lights made a buzzing sound like a living thing. He wondered where all this might be headed. What if the ocularist died? Maybe they could all start over. Maybe Elise would be a part of that.

"Part of what?" his brother said from somewhere.

The muscle in Michael's cheek twitched.

When he came out of the bathroom, he saw the Middle Eastern man behind the counter. His impassive face already granting him forgiveness. Across the room, he could see a couple had already claimed their table. The half-eaten pizza lay between them. How long had he been in the bathroom? He walked over to the video arcade, but it was deserted. Called into the women's bathroom.

"Where is she?" he said to the woman at the table, who looked back at him round-eyed. "Where's the little girl? There was a woman with her," he said. The couple stared back uncomprehendingly. The edges of the room collapsed toward its center. The man behind the counter looked at him strangely. Michael demanded to know where they were, and he shrugged. "Why don't you know?" Michael asked him, pleadingly. The man said Michael was upsetting the customers.

In the front window, unconcerned people loped past. Michael pushed out the door into the cold, then up Broadway, his lungs burning. At the corner of Broadway and Wilson, he called Elise's cell but it went to voice mail. Called his mother's home number and her message machine answered again.

He was the do-right man. He'd stayed quiet, hadn't told them anything. He looked along the street for a sign, any sign. Looked for the white Mercury. Gazed into passing car windows. Taxis. Buses. He bumped into people on the sidewalk. Someone called him a clumsy motherfucker. The L roared overhead.

She was gone.

V

43

ONE NIGHT, AFTER riding his bike back from Deep Eddy Bar, Jack found Kate Ulrich on his darkened porch. When she sat up suddenly, he'd thought of a bird. Alert. Watchful. It took him a moment to recognize her in his fuzzy bike helmet light. She was sitting in a patio chair, stiff, hands over something in her lap.

The ride home had sobered him up some, but he felt unsure of what to do or how to respond. It was as if his muscles had atrophied.

"Can I help in some way?" he said. The headlamp light trembled on the porch windows.

"They are a great comfort," she said in a low, unsteady voice that worried him. "What did you mean by that?" she asked.

"I'm not sure I understand." His heart thudded crazily.

"I have these dreams. But they won't talk to me anymore. They just argue. They're glum. They want something but won't tell me what."

"I see," he said, stupidly.

She pivoted suddenly, asked him about his daughter. He told her she was taking evening courses at the university, unsure where she wanted to go, what she wanted to do. She was working downtown. She'd moved back home with him.

He stood very still.

"They go through that, don't they. All that indecision." Her hands fidgeted over the purse or whatever it was.

"Growing pains," he said.

"Some decisions are made for us, though," she said. "You lost your wife."

"When she died I sort of lost my bearings for a while," he said. "Got confused. I wasn't the best father."

"We always let them down," she said.

"You're right. Then we try to make it up to them." He thought of the new sea green paint, bead board, the smoothness of the sanded floor.

"You know something you're not telling me," she said. She held the purse against her thigh. A comfort, he thought, a totem. In the dim light, her face seemed to narrow, to rid itself of something. His legs grew weak.

What could he tell her? He'd gone into the fire, found them. *Our dream has no bottom.* That was one of the surprises.

"The not knowing is the hardest," she said. "You think if you only knew, you could handle it."

He realized how inadequate he was to this moment.

"You were there," she said.

"I was too late," he said. "I'm always too late." She's tethered me to them in her mind, he thought. She thinks maybe I was the one.

"Elizabeth was terrified of being naked," Kate said.

He found the rope in his head, groped along it. "She was brave," he said.

"I can still smell their hair after a bath." Kate rose from the chair, moved toward the edge of the porch.

"Zadie. She held her hand," he said.

He asked if Kate wanted to come inside, and she said she didn't know. She didn't even know why she'd come. They were quiet for a while. A car two doors down turned into the drive, its lights flaring off the porch. The purse she held had whorls and odd stitching in the leather that reminded him of something.

Kate turned to him. "Take off that bike helmet," she said. "You look ridiculous."

He removed his helmet, then moved around her and unlocked the front door, and she stepped inside.

44

What about the part where I find a video the girls made hamming it up on the stage in Zilker Park? The girls' faces full of delight and mischief—and, sure, maybe they're a little high. How just beneath I can see their adult faces, who they might have been, given a little more time?

What about the part where the girls' school photos arrived in the mail four days after they died? In the photos, they're posed awkwardly, their chins resting on folded hands. Zadie, sensitive about her burn scars, tries to hide them. Elizabeth's left eye squints a little. They'd already arranged to have the photos retaken the next week. The company called me to ask for the additional money. I said, They're gone. You can't have anything more. There was a long silence on the phone. Well, someone there needs to pay, the man said.

45

MICHAEL'S CAR WAS missing. Where it had been was a sign that said SNOW EMERGENCY ROUTE, TOW–AWAY ZONE.

He'd call 911 soon, he told himself, but he needed to think things through first. He walked west on Wilson, toward Clark Street, near where he remembered his mother's neighborhood was. Ravenswood. He liked the sound of it in his head. Something timeless. He dug in his pocket for the scrap of paper with his mother's address. He took deep breaths to slow his heart. Found a corner store and bought a fifth of vodka with the last of his cash. On his way across Wilson Avenue, a passing car slapped his jeans with slush. He found a small park down a side street and drank from the bottle, tried to stop his trembling.

The snow was a rumpled bedsheet in the road.

People plodded by on the sidewalk, their heads gauzy with light from passing cars.

He lit a cigarette and tried Elise's cell phone again.

"What's up?" a man's voice said. It was filled with curiosity. Michael was seized by the image of the older man forking migas into his mouth at Juan in a Million.

"I need to talk to Elise," Michael said. His jaw ached just underneath the pills and vodka.

"Elise? Is there an Elise here?" the man asked someone away from the phone.

"Why are you fucking with me?" Michael said, though he knew why. Knew somehow it would come to this. He saw his daughter curled on a bed in a wood-paneled room somewhere, the harsh glare of a corner streetlight.

A man in a parka sidled up to him. "It's wonderful weather out," he said in a little girl's voice beneath his hood. Michael held the phone tighter, tamped down what was happening.

There was a commotion on the phone. Breathing. "Michael?" Elise's voice said.

"It's me, I'm here," he said. "Who was that?"

"A friend. He thought you were someone else. I'm sorry that we got separated at the restaurant. I got a call from the hospital. Your mother was very upset."

"So you just left?"

"I knocked and knocked on the bathroom door but you didn't come out. So I took Alice with me. Didn't the man behind the counter tell you?"

"Nobody told me anything." There was a clicking sound coming from somewhere far off. Like bird bones snapping.

"My dad's had some kind of relapse. His blood pressure dropped like crazy."

"Put Alice on the phone," Michael said in a voice he didn't recognize.

In front of him, the man in the parka tilted his head and spread his arms wide in a gesture meant to calm Michael. Passing car lights burned in the fur of the man's hood. "A light," the man said, making a smoking motion with his fingers. "And maybe some of what you're having there."

"Daddy?" Alice's voice said on the phone. His legs went limp. "We are playing Zingo."

"Zingo?" His mind tried to pin down what this meant.

"When you win that's what you say."

"So Elise is taking care of you?"

"We're going sledding tomorrow."

"Daddy's coming to get you."

There was a loud crumpling in his ear, and at first Michael thought it was him.

"Michael?" Elise said.

"Is my mom there?" Michael said.

"She's talking with the doctors right now."

"I see."

"I'm worried."

"It's going to be okay," he said, feeling for a second like it might.

"What room?"

"What?"

"Hospital room."

There was a rustling on the phone. "Forty-three twenty-one."

"I'll head over. I'm not far."

"God, Michael, I'm so sorry about all of this."

He hung up, and the man in the parka was still there, looking at him from under the hood. Michael passed him the vodka and he drank a little. "Where you from?" the man asked, wiping his mouth.

"Texas," Michael said.

"Thought I heard some Texas in there when you were talking to your lady."

"My stepsister," he said, and thought how funny that sounded.

"Stepsister?" The man laughed in that mocking but sympathetic way that Andrew always did. Like he'd been there before and would again. Under the parka hood, the man's face bloomed then wilted. "I bet she's fine."

When he got to the hospital, a security man at a desk near the entrance stopped him, looked him over. He could see people waiting near an oncology sign. A couple of kids horsing around near the escalator.

"You got a room number? I'll call up," the security man said. He kept glancing down at Michael's jeans, which were blackened and wet with slush.

He told the man the room number and the man looked blankly at him. "Maybe three twenty-one? That what you mean?"

"Probably I got it wrong. Sorry. It's been a rough night," Michael said.

The man sighed. "Last name?" he said, and dialed the number.

"Stein," Michael said. The ocularist's name sounded strange coming out of his mouth.

Down the hall, two attendants wheeled a gurney into an elevator. The air in the lobby smelled like mouthwash. He tried to remember the last time he'd been in a hospital, and then he remembered Alice's asthma attack when she was two, the marathon evening in the emergency room, nebulizers, suppositories to stop the vomiting. Lucinda's hand on his.

The security man's face hardened. "No Stein," he said, hanging up the phone. "People in that room named Taylor."

"Must be some mistake," Michael said, grinding his teeth. He
tried to smile at the man.

"Yes," the security man said, "there must be." He glanced off
at the reception counter, where people sat upright but seemed
asleep. He rested his hands on his belt, where a radio hung.

"Maybe I could go up and speak with somebody."

"Can't let you up there unless you've got a room. Unless you
got family."

Where were they? What kind of game was Elise playing? He
called her again on his cell but it clicked over to voice mail.

Outside, in the semicircle drive, snow swirled.

His jean pants legs had frozen stiff. He worried about hypothermia.
He'd get warm at his mother's place, dry off. What size pants did
the ocularist wear? he wondered. At the corner of Wilson and Ash-
land, he saw a temple of some sort. Along its eaves, large banners
strewn with a jumble of Chinese characters. A twenty-foot Buddha
smiled an indecipherable smile from behind the wrought-iron
fence, snow nestling in the crook of his raised arm.

He turned left at Paulina and found the lit porch of his mother's
house. It seemed less regal than the one in his mind, a little run-
down. A porch swing hung slightly askew. He knocked and rang
the doorbell but no one answered. He couldn't feel his hands. He
looked in the front window. A light burned in the hallway. He
thought he could hear a TV or radio on somewhere. He knocked
again, louder. He went around the house, kicked at the back of the
gate, which was wedged shut with ice, and when it gave way, he

went around to the tiny square of backyard. Something in the backyard seemed to muffle the sounds of the traffic, the crowdedness of the city. He tried the back door but it was locked. He looked through the window of the garage, which was off an alley, but there was no car. His bowels knotted. He picked up a hand spade from a stone planter and broke out a window panel on the back door, reached in and opened it. He stepped inside and the grinding of glass under his feet seemed to echo through his mother's house.

46

J ACK DIDN'T KNOW what to make of it. The first night, he felt ashamed.

In his kitchen, Kate Ulrich kissed him hard and pressed him up against the counter. Then they found their way into the living room, struggled with their clothes. She unbuckled his belt, he fumbled with her jean button, her top. They fucked on the floor rug until his knees were raw, then she straddled him in a chair. She shouted obscenities at him through gritted teeth. Bit his lip, drew blood. She panted so wildly, he thought she might pass out. Just before he came, she rose off him in the chair and went to hide from him in the house. Forced him to find her. They fucked on the laundry room floor, on a pile of dirty clothes.

Sometime in the early morning, Samantha came home from work and Kate gathered her clothes, dressed hurriedly, and left.

The next night, he left a key for her. The lights were off in the house when he got home. After searching the rooms, he found her naked in his bedroom closet behind secondhand suits his wife had bought for him. She demanded that he bind her hands to the bed frame with his neckties. She demanded that he strap his bike helmet light to the bedpost. Her leather purse with its whorls and stitching sat on the bedside table. There was a fierceness to her that made him afraid. Her arms strained at the bindings, though he knew he'd tied them loosely enough for her to pull her wrists out. Sweat gathered between her breasts. She panted and shouted. Blood thrummed in his head. The bed narrowed, collapsed into the backseat of a car lit by dashboard lights. Kate's eyes fixed on him but on some singular point beyond him, too. And then it was as if he were looking through her eyes at himself, his tensed and baffled face. And everything inside him grew hot, dark, and wet.

The next morning, Sam got up late as usual. She slunk into the living room in her robe, waved limply at him, rubbed her eyes. Jack was drinking coffee at the kitchen table when he saw her poke at something under the couch with her bare foot. She slid it out with her toes. A black lace bra. "Ooh–la–la," she said.

47

I T WAS LATE when they got back to the house, and the first thing Kay noticed was a light on in the kitchen. She and her husband, Bob, had been downtown in the Loop all day, a celebratory lunch with Elise at the Gage and then graduation, which had run late, with Senator Durbin's speech going on and on. Elise's boyfriend, Josh, had come. Tattoos everywhere. The illustrated man. The beard made him seem older, more sure of himself than he was. Still, she thought, he was pleasant enough. Had his charms. A fiction writing student (unemployed). He liked South American writers. They'd talked a little at lunch about the Chilean writer Roberto Bolaño. She would introduce Michael to them after he and Alice drove in tomorrow, something low-key. Try to get Michael to focus on something other than his impending divorce. Life went on, she thought, despite everything.

Coming up the back steps, she noticed the broken glass, the jagged opening where the pane in the door had been. She called to Bob. Over the summer, someone had broken into the garage, stolen their bikes. Even took the time to switch out one set of tires for better ones. "Don't go into the house," Bob said. "Absolutely do not go in." He slogged through snow, went up on his toes, and peered through back windows. A short man, Bob, though she hardly ever noticed. At the back door, he poked his cell phone through the broken pane, shone it along the floor and wall. Glass on the floor, he said, maybe some blood. He stood there on the porch steps, chewed his lip. Detective Bob. Circumspect. Taciturn. Her protector.

Through the broken pane, she could see their home phone's green message light blinking in the hallway.

They waited on the police for ten minutes or so. When the police finally pulled up in front, lights flashing, Bob said, maybe he should go in with them, take a look around. He started to say something else, something brave and useless, but she put a hand to his chest. He laughed.

48

W HAT ROSA KNEW:
The man had worked at the Driskill Hotel for two
years under the name Eugene Dudaev. He'd been a concierge for a
time. Then he worked in hospitality, managing banquets and the
like. Weddings, graduation parties, quinceañeras. Some people
recalled that in the winter he wore a fashionable wool overcoat.
Others said he was formal but not stiff. A few were struck by his
knowledge of the hotel's long history, Austin's natural landscape. He
seemed younger than he was, they said. A few others said there was
some mistake, that the Dudaev they knew had a thick Russian accent,
was in his fifties, and had immigrated from Chechnya during the
height of the separatist war there. He had children, they believed, still
living there and perhaps that's why he left the hotel, to go back.

Still others on the hospitality staff (who refused to be quoted) said
they had misgivings about him. That he'd taken up with two of the
young Mexican housekeepers (he also spoke Spanish) and that both
women had quit abruptly, without giving notice. Dudaev left the
hotel soon after the second housekeeper quit five months before,
leaving no forwarding address. When Rosa found a photo of Dudaev
on the Internet, he was bearded, thick-necked, and balding.

The two young women, the staff said, were unlucky.

49

ONE NIGHT WHEN Jack slept at the fire station, Kate used her key and swaddled her head in white wine and old TV shows in his living room. *The Dick Van Dyke Show,* her favorite, was on. She'd watched it with the girls years before on *Nick at Night.* In the introduction to every episode Rob would trip and fall spectacularly over the living room ottoman. They made an alternative beginning, too—at the last second Rob notices the ottoman and steps gracefully around it. Everyone laughs.

"What are you doing here?" Sam said from the entryway. Sam was in her all-black waitress getup. A thief or assassin, Kate thought underneath her wine. Sam's braided hair hung over one shoulder. Behind her was a tall young man with Civil War side-burns, dressed the same. They'd been groping and kissing in the hallway. Kate had heard them in the dark. "I should go," the young man said, moving toward the door, but Sam grabbed his arm.

"You two look like you'd steal us blind," Kate said. "Or slit our throats while we slept."

"You're up late," Sam said, narrowing her eyes at Kate. She readjusted her shirt.

"Insomnia," Kate said. "My mother had it."

"Is insomnia hereditary?" Sam said, tilting her head in her funny assassin way.

"Most things are," Kate said. *This girl,* she thought.

Kate grabbed glasses from the kitchen and poured the couple some wine, and they sat with her to watch an episode of *Dick Van Dyke*. Danny Thomas was in it. He was an alien. It was all a dream.

The young man—his name was Lonnie—smiled conspiratorially at Kate and said he'd seen this one. He pulled at his sideburns. A good sport, Kate thought.

Kate asked Sam about their night (terrible, Sam said, someone had stolen half her tips from behind the bar); what they were planning to do for the weekend (camping at Pedernales State Park); the film course Sam was taking (Cassavetes's seventies work was so interesting); and if they thought she was crazy (Kate only asked this in her head).

Sam played with her braid.

In the dim light of the hallway, Kate could see her own brood gathering there on the wall, filling all the empty space. Their heads bent toward the invisible radio they spoke through.

"How about you and Dad?" Sam looked over at the young man when she said this. He raised his eyebrows, smiled into his shirt.

"We're such homebodies," Kate said. Shrugged an exaggerated shrug. "Your dad still has work to do around here. The bead board needs staining." She tipped her wineglass toward the living room wall.

After a while, the young man's head bobbed, nodding off. *Baby-necking,* Kate remembered her girls calling it.

Sam ruthlessly appraised her from the end of the couch.

Lonnie was asleep now, his head back against the cushion.

"He seems interesting," Kate said, in what she thought was a whisper.

Something softened in Sam's face. Maybe just a tiredness creeping in, Kate thought. Tiredness made you open to more things. She and Sam had so much in common, hadn't they? Sam always missing her mother.

"He's funny," Sam said, and seemed to remember something Lonnie had said on the way that made her laugh. Color rose in Sam's face and neck from the wine.

Her girls would be about Sam's age now. Making all her same mistakes. Everything contingent, everything forgiven, she thought. She wanted the unending worry back. She wanted to hurt in all the right ways.

Her girls called to her from the hallway.

Kate rose off the couch to head for bed. "Good night, good night," she told Sam in a singsongy voice, and leaned in to kiss her cheek. But she held Sam instead, smelled her hair. Electricity crackled in the room. She would close the gap. She would love her as her own.

Sam pulled away.

50

What about the part where a year after they died, late at night, I spray-painted their names on the Lamar Street Bridge? ELIZABETH. ZADIE. MEREDITH. *(I'd stopped making her a white space on the wall.) Imagined people passing beneath in cars, speaking their names. Elizabeth. Zadie. Meredith. Kids in the backseat wanting an explanation. Who are these girls? What has become of them? And a story would have to be told, but it would be missing so many things because we've already begun to forget, and so we cling to all the half-remembered bits — a line from a song they'd sung, the smell of their skin, small bruises on their arms after a vaccination — and then we find we've bound them up in all these half-remembered things, and bound ourselves, too, and our heart keeps beating but only sends itself away and returns to itself, and then it isn't a story at all but only beads strung along a necklace, a measuring-out of days.*

51

ROSA IS HEADED north on the L to see an old friend from college. The wheels squeal on the track. The snow makes things seem quieter when they're not, she thinks. The train crosses the bridge at the river, curves between buildings where you can see people from time to time in their kitchens, making dinner, or drinking alone, or kissing in a stairwell, lit from behind like in a movie. She loved this about Chicago. That it went on with its business, no matter. She remembered once, years ago, riding the L with her dad and the train stopping for twenty minutes on the tracks for a man who was threatening to kill himself. People eventually got out and walked and made a point of telling the man what they thought as they passed on the plat-form catwalk above. "Lesson number one," a man yelled down to him. "You gonna do something, do it right. Don't pussyfoot around."

Her dad was going to need someone here to help out over the next few months. Surgery and recovery and radiation. And then what? She'd be flying back and forth, she expected. She couldn't be sure he was even being straight with her. There would need to be more consultations. It was hard to see very far ahead.

The old friend she was meeting lived off Montrose Avenue,

near a park. They'd gone to Loyola together. The friend, Jess, now had two girls, eight and ten. She still did some reporting here and there. Human interest stuff in the 'burbs for the *Tribune* supplements. Keeping a foot in the door, she said. Rosa had almost forgotten that her ex-boyfriend David had been the one who'd introduced them their sophomore year.

David, who, a year after she broke things off and four months after she'd gotten a restraining order after all the calls and threats, had gotten into her Austin apartment building on false pretenses, made his way upstairs, broken into the apartment he assumed was hers, and lay down in the bed. Then he'd poured camping lantern fuel over himself and set himself on fire.

Somehow he'd gotten her apartment number wrong. No one was home. Rosa had heard the banging and smelled the smoke, and they'd evacuated the building. Water from the fire hoses rolled down the stairs and pooled in the lobby. A fatality, the police said later. A man had set fire to himself. The next morning the building super, who knew about the restraining order, told her it had been David and she remembered the acrid smell.

She'd been lucky, was all. A transposed number in his head, like so many other chance events in her life and in the lives of those she wrote about and cared for. Eventually these events— the good and the bad—would seem inevitable. Would be claimed, finally, as their own by those who lived them, like lost children.

As the L slowed at a curve, she could see people moving inside the building next to them, dancing in gym clothes and leotards, and for a moment their figures were joined with the reflected figures and faces on the train.

Twenty minutes later, as she stepped off the train and onto the platform, she saw flashing lights below, a knot of cops and EMTs at the corner in front of a bakery. A half dozen police cruisers parked along the snowy street. Police tape. She was thankful she didn't have to report what it was or who was hurt or what it might mean for those who would try to get beyond it.

She thought vaguely of the blue crate at home in Austin, its photos, interview tapes, transcripts, and false leads. The person of interest who'd apparently fled the state. Hollis Finger, the young man in the coat, the anonymous caller. All separate but somehow tied to one another. Like elements from a collective dream.

She saw the girls' faces from the billboard. Her throat tightened.

It was colder out now, and she was glad it was only a short walk to the restaurant where her friend waited.

52

MICHAEL HAD FALLEN asleep on his mother's bed and then woken to men's voices downstairs. It took him a few seconds to get his bearings. On the bedside table, old photos of him and Andrew. Alice's school photo from last year. Several others of Elise, he supposed. She looked nothing like the woman he'd met at the pizzeria. Dark eyes. A slight gap between her front teeth. He thought of Lucinda's threats. Had she hired the other woman to take Alice?

The image of Alice in the wood-paneled room came back to him.

Blue and white lights tumbled on the ceiling.

He rose off the bed, thought about the bathroom, then decided on the closet, slid open the louvered doors and crouched in the back among his mother's hanging dresses and luggage. Against his face, a gauzy dress fabric, a mask, a shroud. He could hear the heat kick on.

He'd called his dad and Margo earlier but had gotten Olive, Margo's mother. She said Margo was resting. "She has conceived," Olive said. He said, yes, he remembered. "Is Darnell there?" he asked, something hard rising up in his chest. There was a fumbling on the phone. "Do you know what it is to be a woman?" Olive asked him. And then the phone went dead.

His brother whispered something unintelligible in his ear.

He was the do-right man.

When the men came up the stairs, they carried Michael's mother's voice up with them. They heaved the weight of it room to room, looking for him, their feet creaking on the wood. And when he rose up from his hiding place and his legs moved with infinite slowness toward the door and into the hall, then down the stairs and across the living room, he felt an odd pulling just below his stomach and imagined, in the seconds before he plunged out the front door into the bitter cold and shifting light, an umbilical cord trailing behind. He ran across yards, jumped over walls and fences. After a few blocks, his legs began to cramp. He came out of an alley, turned up Montrose Avenue toward the brightly lit L.

They found him in front of a small bakery. A police car cut him off at the corner and the officers inside leaped out and chased him. They didn't even know who he was. It didn't matter. They caught him by his umbilical, slung him to the snowy ground.

When he tried to tell them that it was all a mistake, what he said made no sense. One of the officers Tasered him as he rose off the ground, and his body ignited and he could see the branching veins at the back of his retina. But to his great surprise he could still move, as if there was a bad connection, as if his body was wired wrong. He flung an arm up to ward off what was coming and struck one of the officers in the face. And then something unbearably hard shattered his ribs on his left side. And he heard one of the officers shout that he'd better get the fuck down, and, as he was retching in the snow from the pain, he thought how strange it was that the officer couldn't see that he *was* down.

Above him, one of the officers fumbled with the Taser, cursing its unreliability. The second time Michael rose, he thought he saw, at the edge of his vision, his mother's old Buick station wagon that she'd traded in years ago, pull to the curb. The front passenger door was open and there beside his mother on the seat sat Alice, looking out at him with great curiosity. And in her eyes was the boundless lake.

Beyond them, down the street, the L platform gleamed. He could hear a train approaching.

When one of the officers grabbed his shoulder, Michael clutched at the man's jacket, his belt, spun himself loose. The officer grimaced and grabbed his own neck. Blood was on the snow. Michael stood in front of the bakery windows, his breath pluming, the officer's utility knife in his hand. And then Michael knew the man staggering there was his brother and that the blood on the snow was his blood and Michael moved toward him to carry his burden. And the other officer raised his gun and shot Michael in the chest.

53

KATE IS FEELING her way along a rope. Down in all that dark and smoke and water. It's not a place to be but a place to not be. She knows this. Even so, she's here. Every so often she feels a knot, a knuckle along a spine. Every so often she feels a small tug at the other end. There's a tip-of-the-tongue taste of something sweet in the air. Her heart beats faster.

She's groping along like this for hours, it seems, ankle-deep in water. And then the rope, which she'll still feel between her hands when she wakes, comes to an end.

54

T HIS IS WHAT Darnell imagines:

In a movie, the director would use a jump-cut shot to compress time and heighten tension: the father character (early fifties, graying) working in his woodshop with a skill saw and lathe. Sawdust in the air. He's wearing earplugs, so instead of the tool's high-pitched whine we hear only a distant humming. He won't hear the detectives knocking at his front door or calling his cell phone. The father is building something in the shape of something else, a movie prop. A Comanche bow or a roadhouse sign or a weathervane. A likeness to anchor the movie in time and space. Here we might see a cutaway shot of the father's hands at work—callused, sun-freckled. His hands the steadying forces of his life, you'd think. Never still. Then we'd pull in close: the father's face concentrated, eyes behind protective glasses narrowed to blade and board, the penciled line where they meet. Closer still, an eye fills the screen and we see, reflected in its blue iris, tiny particles of sawdust that whirl about his face. Inside the iris, these particles miraculously recombine to form a younger, dark-haired version of the father and his former wife down on their knees, giving their two boys a bath. The boys—three and six—make faces, splash water out of the tub. The younger one is fussy, ready for bed. The older one, always testing them, is climbing out. The boys' mother—arms outstretched—tries to coax him back into the tub. The father leans back from all the splashing, the commotion, turns his head. A bemused smile on his face. He could be any father, really, helping out with the kids at the end of the day. Fears and hopes roiling through him. We might see in the father's turning away, his bemused smile, something portentous. But the father and his family aren't watching the movie; they're in it. They're not even aware yet of the forces tugging at them. How one thing will pull another along. Floating there in the father's iris, the rest of their lives can't be imagined.

55

MARGO LEANS AGAINST a pillar in the pool bath-
house, braces for the next contraction. The limestone is
cool against her face. She's left her cell phone in her knit bag down
by the Springs. She often swims her laps here alone after closing
to avoid the crowds. She'd begun to feel more buoyant in her seventh month, despite her doctor's warnings about hypertension. As
if the baby is making slow peace with inside becoming outside.
Water seeking its own level. But right now her bowels are filling
with concrete. Panting here in the dusky light, she's seized by the
thought that Darnell has done this to her—scooped pails of sand
from the collapsed backyard sandbox, mixed it, and spoon-fed her
in bed. She'd tried to say something to him about it, but her
tongue was stifled by the spoon, her teeth grinding against grit.
Just a little more, Darnell would say. To keep up your strength.
He'd touched the side of her cheek with the spoon to get her to
open, the way you'd do a baby. Darnell was patient. He was building a monument to patience inside her bowels. Patience abides. Its
weight holding you steady and balanced in the water, like ballast
for a ship.

But then it isn't Darnell at all, who she knows she'll soon leave.
It isn't Darnell's sons' undoing, isn't her worry over Alice back

with her unsteady mother, or Margo's own mother and father, fading quickly now, paper-thin versions of the people they'd been. It isn't Kate, who'd called her about Michael that morning, her voice a mix of sympathy and accusation. Who was it then, filling her up this way?

The next contraction hits, doubles her over. She steadies herself against the pillar. Calls out. Someone will hear, she thinks, someone will come. One of her fingernails bites into the flesh of her palm, but she hardly notices. And it occurs to her that it's her own doing. That she's filled up with herself but will always feel empty. It's a sleight of hand. A box with a false-bottom mirror where you could hide anything. How could she have forgotten? She's conceived herself.

Her breath comes in great heaves now. In the bruised last-light, she leans against the pillar in the great temple knowing she can bring it down or hold it up — it's up to her. Only she is left to tell the tale.

56

IN SAM'S DREAM, her mother is swinging an aluminum baseball bat through their house. She smashes the bay windows in the den and then the tall windows in the living room. She shatters the antique chandelier she'd bought on a trip to Houston soon after she married Sam's dad, one that still hangs in their house. She explodes the sconce lights and the stained glass in the hallway. In life, in the throes of her aneurysm, she'd only broken out the three bay windows in the den. In the dream, she spares nothing. Her mother is deliberate, thoughtful as she goes along, a quality Sam thinks admirable and lacking in herself. Sam is vaguely aware of the chaos raging in her mother's brain, which in the dream sounded like a crazed Geiger counter. Her mother moves through the house but reads to her in the voice of Sam's third-grade teacher, Mrs. Swatzel. *Little House in the Big Woods.* Pa and the bear. Her mother, who is also Mrs. Swatzel, goes on smashing with the bat, pausing only to readjust the crossing-guard sash Mrs. Swatzel used to wear after school. In life, everyone wondered: Had her mother shattered the windows out of anger? Frustration? The random heat lightning in her brain? No one knew. They found her sprawled on the kitchen floor one morning after a jogger passing the house had heard the ruckus, seen the jagged openings.

Someone had called her dad at the station. At first they'd thought there had been a break-in, an intruder. Wasn't that what the base-ball bat in the hallway closet was for?

In the dream, her mother pauses between one window and the next, and despite the Geiger counter noise turns to Sam and says, *See? I'm calling to you. I can't speak anymore, can't dial a phone, can't even think straight. But I'm calling to you.* Her mother seems elated at the news. *You will hear me. These are the shouts of my body. This is how I love you.*

57

KATE'S EX-HUSBAND RAY is still here, and sometimes that's enough. Other days, his failures haunt him. He has a maintenance job for the park district and he drives one of the groundskeeper carts along the hike and bike trail, taking care of small repairs, cleaning up after park events, removing graffiti from bridges and benches. He likes the solitude and the city benefits. Doesn't like the swollen ankles or the heat, which he's grown less tolerant of. He often thinks of Kate and the girls. A life he once had that now seems like someone else's. He'd gone to the girls' anniversary vigils but had grown a beard for the occasions, stood anonymously in the back, and left early. He knew Kate had moved into one of the condos downtown that he and Kate used to make fun of. *Boondoggles,* they'd called them. *Californication.* Months ago, he'd gotten her number from a friend (who advised him, of course, not to contact her) and called Kate. He wanted to tell her that he knew he'd failed them. That maybe if he'd been there, he could have prevented it. That he carries the weight of those forty-seven missing minutes like a stone in his belly. But when he called, he didn't say anything, just listened to her voice saying *hello hello who's this?* and for some reason thought of a bird, its head jerking this way and that. He remembered a wren once getting into the house and he and the girls had closed the curtains and turned off all the lights, and Kate held the cat in her arms, until, in the dark, the wren grew calmer and he placed a towel over it. *Silly old bird thinks it's night,* Elizabeth had said, delighted. On the phone, Kate said, "Jack, is this you?" When Ray didn't say anything, she hung up.

Ray is near the hike and bike trail on Riverside Drive when he sees the fat man on the train trestle that crosses the river. On night shifts, he sometimes chases off kids or drunk university students trying to climb it. He calls his supervisor, says someone's up on the trestle, maybe a prank, maybe a jumper, hard to tell. He waits but nobody comes, no supervisor, no cop, no siren. The man seems to be frozen up there, staring down at the water. Ray calls up at him. Nothing. Swallows dive around one of the trestle piers. So Ray climbs up, despite his bad ankles and fear of heights, goes out on the trestle, thinking maybe he can talk him down. From up top he can see most of the park and bike path. The high-rises across the river loom over him. When he gets about thirty feet away, he can see that the man is barefoot, his pants rolled up like he's wading in a creek or in the surf. His shoes are draped around his neck by their laces. He turns toward Ray, calm, like he expected Ray would be along any minute. Is the fishing any good here? the fat man asks. He peers down as if he's watching a school of them dart around. Ray explains the trestle is off-limits, asks if he can help him, you know, get down. The fat man says maybe so, maybe so. He wants to tell

Ray something but first he needs to know a few things, for instance, what was the exact distance from the trestle to the water's surface? Ray thinks: Just my luck, bat-shit crazy and I stumble on him. Ray tells him he's only here to be sure the man gets down safe. He appreciates that, the fat man says. Then he doesn't say anything but Ray can see his wheels are turning. The fat man says he's fond of weights and measurements. They can tell you the shape of something even if you never saw it. Consider this trestle, he says, and leans out, the metal rail disappearing into his big gut. Ray shoots forward, his heart thudding. But the fat man just eyes the girders and supports down there. Points to this and that. Says something about spandrels and cables and the weight of the thing. All this, he says, only ideas, measurements in a person's head before it's built.

Ray looks for his supervisor, a cop car. The sun glares off all that high-rise glass. Heat's coming on. Ray moves closer to the fat man, but the height is starting to make him dizzy, a little wobbly in the legs.

The fat man says he worked as an assistant engineer for Amtrak for many years, had ridden over hundreds of bridges like this. Ridden across them on the City of New Orleans, which nightly bisected the country from Chicago down through the South. Crossed the five-hundred-foot Pit River Bridge in California, the tallest cantilever train bridge in the world, which also lured the desperate and forlorn. A bridge, the fat man says, is made in the pattern of man, his insides. Cables and trusses, sinew and bone. But, of course, a bridge is also a pattern of the void it spans. Where they touch.

That's something, Ray says, because he doesn't know what to say to that.

I was fond of that life, the fat man says.

Well, we're all fond of life, Ray says.

Ray can see the man is measuring something in his head.

When I was a young boy, the man says, on summer days my friends and I used to climb up this trestle. We'd crouch down on the beams just underneath the tracks. When the train came, there would be a terrible roaring and grinding over us and the sun would be blotted out. The refrigerated cars would pass over and cold water from the condensation would rain down through the timbers. We were quite fond of that. The shock of it. The way it would throw you out of yourself and bring you back again.

The fat man shifts his weight from one foot to the other, his toes as big as spoons.

Ray can hear a siren. Cottonwoods tremble along the river-bank. Something is happening. Ray's legs go wobbly again. There will be questions about why he didn't do more, he thinks. Why he wasn't more persistent or persuasive. Why he wasn't more capable. Why he wasn't someone else.

The fat man looks out over the river, shoes yoked around his neck, says he's never actually been on this train trestle in his life before now. Never been an assistant engineer. Why I tell such lies, I don't know, he says. He rises up on his toes, grips the sides, and heaves one meaty leg over. The metal seems to groan under him. Then, just as the man is about to go over—and this is the hardest part for Ray to understand—Ray throws himself at the man's

other leg. Grabs him around the thigh, the size of a normal man's
torso. Buries his face in it. The fat man is straddling the trestle
wall now. Poised between two worlds. He struggles and twists.
Ray's head hits something hard, once, twice. There's a roaring in
his ears. But he doesn't let go.

58

J ACK AND SAM went to see a double feature of *To Have and Have Not* and *Key Largo* at the Paramount Theatre. Sam had gotten a job there that spring at the concession stand. She loved the thick red velvet curtains, the elderly ushers in their uniforms. The timeless feel of the place. On their way in, Jack had spotted Kate in the lobby with Edward, who he'd met at the Christmas party. Jack said hello and they talked a bit about Kate's new job at a realty company. Sam was friendly but kept her distance. He wanted to ask Kate what the detectives had told her, about the death of the man in Chicago, but he stuck to small talk. Likely the murders would remain unsolved, as the reports said. But maybe now she might get on with things, build a new life. Would he? Talking with her now, a part of him still held out hope.

The last time he and Kate had been together, more than two months ago, she slept beside him in bed, the sheet twisted between her thighs. A pale C-section scar above her pubic bone, faint stretch marks along her breasts, hips. Her freckled shoulder, the shell of her ear. He cupped her hip with his hand as if to test if she were real. And he marveled at being there with her then, in that moment, among the many that might not have been. Tethered to

each other. Through grief? Solace? Did it matter? And for a minute or so it seemed that moment would never pass. *Our dream has
no bottom.* And lying there beside her, his hand still on her hip, he
heard the newspaper hit the bushes outside the window, and after
a little while, the sprinkler start up. And then Sam pulled into the
driveway, her headlights flaring off the back wall, and Kate jerked
awake beside him.

59

HOLLIS FINGER CROSSES Barton Springs Road in the backhoe he's stolen from a condo construction site. In Iraq, he'd driven military trucks and even operated a small crane, and this wasn't so different. True, he had some trouble at the bridge when a tread caught a fire hydrant at the curb and then scraped the corner of the bridge wall, but he'd made it through. The caterwauling of the engines and the condition of the seat cushion—stained, lumpy with moisture—unsettle him. Remain calm, he thinks. *I have carved you on the palm of my hand.*

At the edge of the park, he sees birds—starlings—wheeling after insects around the moon tower. Before him, an expanse of dew-thick grass, rising and falling, like sea swells.

The true moon arcs over the trees. The false one moves through him like a tide. He lifts rock, soil, and root. He heaves great trees from the ground. He digs deep. Shatters water and utility pipes, colorful maps of which are etched in his head. The shovel groans at its work. Debris, dust flies. The glass cage that houses him grows fissures until his vision is like that of an insect. He is a jealous guardian, a faithful slave, a doting father, an innocent son. He is Abraham and Isaac, wielding the knife above while welcoming it to his throat. And before they lay hands upon Hollis, before he's dragged from his glass box and beaten by God's unwitting fists, he carves the girls' likeness into the earth.

60

TWO BLOCKS FROM our Nana's place, there's an abandoned house near the beach that will one day burn down. But that part doesn't matter yet.

We are eleven and twelve. We don't see our horsey girl as much since her parents divorced, since she moves back and forth. We're upset. Moody. Vengeful. There's another man involved, we're sure of it, we tell her. How could her mother do this to him? To Mister Lopez, with the kindly face, who never raises his voice except for that time when we get into his stash? We try not to talk this way unless we need to put our horsey girl in her place.

The stakes seem higher now when we're together. So we try to make it count.

At the abandoned house near our Nana's, we use a screwdriver to pry loose the wood from the bay window where the stained glass used to be. Inside, despite the mess, everything is as it once was—in the sink a shriveled-up bar of Dial soap, seventies stickers stuck to the back of the bathroom door (KEEP ON TRUCKIN'!). In the sink, lime green plates thick with muck. A few shattered on the floor. A fogged glass pitcher on the table we imagine filled with Tang, the drink of astronauts. On the counter, a Rotary Club cookbook, opened to Chicken Cordon Bleu. Old clothes cover the bedroom floor three inches thick—dresses, blazers, pants, underwear, bras, all blackened with mildew and rot from leaks in a ceiling that looks like a bubbling upside-down sea. In the middle of the bedroom, a pyramid of shoes rises that reminds us of something that hasn't happened yet. In another bedroom, filled with old luggage, a polished wood baby crib. Something passed down that won't go any further.

The place won't last much longer. Someone has already blackened a living room wall by starting a fire where the fake fireplace is. Someone stole whatever valuables the family had years ago from the dresser drawers, cabinets, and jewelry box. Still, they missed a few things. Some photos taken on the beach where a Mexican-looking woman (*swarthy!* our horsey girl says) in a two-piece and a wiry man roll in the surf *From Here to Eternity*–style. (The oldest of us shows how it's done, arms hugging herself, but rolls into the tide of rotted, mildewed clothes.) In one photo, a girl about our age is eyeing the man and woman, her mouth opened into a shriek or a laugh. We imagine she's their daughter, surprised and embarrassed to find her parents are still in love after all these years. The youngest of us stuffs the photos in her pocket.

Other keepsakes are left behind. On top of a kitchen door-frame, we find a three-legged cast-iron horse with a Civil War rider. In a wool coat pocket, a makeup compact with powder still inside. A shellacked horned frog in a desk drawer. On a medicine cabinet shelf, among bottles of Campho-Phenique and yellowed Q-tips, a thin silver ring engraved with ALWAYS LOVE ANTOINE. A plea or a promise? Discuss.

As our Nana says, *the mind reels.* Where did these people go so suddenly without their keepsakes? Without their Chicken

Cordon Bleu? Or shellacked horned frog? Were they told to leave this place or else? Were they cursed? Did their luck turn against them? Or maybe, just maybe, did they get lucky? Did they leave before whatever was coming got here?

We find old bills from JCPenney and Texaco. Timothy Crabtree is the man. Carmona Exposito, the woman. We piece it together in our heads. Tim and Carmona put their feet up by the fake fireplace, make their plans. We call the daughter we've given them Nina. Nina Exposito. We like the sound. Sexy, like an international assassin. Our horsey girl says Exposito is Spanish for "orphan." Foundling. Abandoned, but taken in. You just look up one day and there she is down among the duckweed and cattails. Thick eyelashes and dark skin. *Swarthy,* our horsey girl says.

When we bring our keepsakes back in a cigar box we found (we imagine Nina smoking cigarillos), our Nana is quiet for a while. Then she tells us a story we never used to listen to, about her mother, whose family abandoned their house in Poland, just before the war. Just before the Nazis came. Everything left just as it was. Our Nana's mother, only seventeen at the time, obsessed all her life with the things they'd left behind. She'd dream of strangers ransacking the place. But then one day—isn't it always "but then one day" in these stories?—our Nana's mother had a dream about a woman, a stranger combing a little girl's hair with a left-behind whalebone comb, the one our Nana's mother had combed her own hair with, hair that at the time of the dream had been falling out in the sink. It made our Nana's mother happy that these things had gone on without her, that they had a life of their own.

The clock ticks loud and slow in our Nana's kitchen.

Our Nana lifts the cigar box lid again and again, as if she expects to find something different inside each time.

See the abandoned house? See the flames roll over the clothes along the floor, leap to gauzy curtains? See the wallpaper blacken and curl? See the bindings and ligatures ignite?

We're not here. We've taken our things and gone.

Acknowledgments

I'm especially grateful to Tommi Ferguson for her guidance, vision, patience, and love. And to Ethan Bassoff and Pat Strachan, without whom...

Heartfelt thanks to Dean Blackwood, Scott Stebler, Ben Fountain, Miles Harvey, Jordan Smith, Rosa Eberly, Janet Burroway, Jarrett Dapier, Ellie Blackwood, Darren Defrain, Debra Monroe, Elizabeth Taylor, and Jill Meyers, who generously read early and late versions of *See How Small* and helped improve it.

To my parents, Anita and Bob Gatchel and Bill and Lois Blackwood, for their love and generosity.

And special thanks to the Whiting Foundation, The Texas Institute of Letters, everyone at Little, Brown and Company, and to my colleagues and students at Roosevelt University and Southern Illinois University–Carbondale.

About the Author

SCOTT BLACKWOOD is the author of two previous books of fiction, *In the Shadow of Our House* and *We Agreed to Meet Just Here,* and a recipient of a 2011 Whiting Writers' Award. A longtime resident of Austin, Texas, Blackwood now lives in Chicago.